THE DRAGON OF HOPE ISLAND

science fiction novel by

Wentworth M Johnson

I & W Johnson Books

This book is dedicated to

Denis George Bowers (12 August 1947 – 30 November 2001)

'You have power over your mind - not outside events. Realize this, and you will find strength.'

MARCUS AURELIUS   26 APRIL 121 - 17 MARCH 180

CONTENTS

KIDNAPPED

Chapter 1

Death leapt from the mountaintop, striking the flimsy aircraft and sending it spiralling to its doom. Peace and tranquility returned to the passive blue ocean. Only a wispy trail of smoke drifted by, betraying the disastrous event that had just transpired.

"Interesting, no?"

Peter looked up at the gold-toothed grinning China-man. "Interesting? Yeah! I guess so. But it's just a story."

"Ah, you do not believe. No?"

Peter smiled. "It's a little too far-fetched and well ... should I say more like science fiction."

"Mr. Chan, I believe. Yes, I truly believe."

"We're not flying on that route now, are we?"

The China-man grinned and sat on the seat next to Peter. With a broad smile, he said, "There are many stories of the Banda Sea Triangle, Mr. Chan. Should I say, there is no smoke without the fire? Is that not true?"

Peter's countenance brightened. "I am a scientist. I deal only with facts, cold hard facts. The tales of fishermen are just that, fishermen's tales. There are no monsters in the Banda Sea, or for that matter, any other ocean, triangular or otherwise."

The China-man took one of Peter's hands and in a soft,

warm voice said, "The most fascinating story is from a New Zealand newspaper of 1949. It was reported that a New Guinea fisherman said he saw Amelia Earhart's Lockheed 10E passing near an island known locally as 'Dragon's Nest'. He said a bolt of light leapt from the pinnacle of the island and totally destroyed the machine. Do you think, Mr. Chan, that an ignorant fisherman could invent such a preposterous tale?"

"Anyone can lie."

"True, Mr. Chan, but to what end? Why would a lowly fisherman makeup such a story?"

Thoughtfully Peter scratched his ear pondering the question for a moment. "I don't know. I will have to think about it, but as I said, anyone can tell lies."

With no further conversation, the China-man left the young American scientist to his deep thoughts. The reported encounter had several strange aspects. As the flight attendant passed Peter, he attracted her attention. "Excuse me, miss, did you see that gentleman sitting here with me a moment ago?"

"Yes, Mr. Chan, he was commander Soo-Lin, our reserve pilot."

"Oh! How is it that everyone on this flight seems to know my name?"

She smiled delightfully. "Everyone knows of Mr. Chan. You are famous, sir."

The PA announced that the aircraft would soon be landing in Singapore. Trembling with excitement and anticipation, Peter peered eagerly through the window to get a first glimpse of his new home. Air turbulence increased as the plane descended over the dark sea. The lights of Singapore city became visible, shining like a beautiful jewel against the blackness of the ocean. With a bump and a squeal of tires, the giant plane touched down and began its run down the long taxiway. Surprisingly, Peter found the airport as modern as any in America. He'd expected something quite unfamiliar. The cleanliness, efficiency, and automation seemed out of place.

Customs and immigration were little more than a

formality. As soon as he was in the reception area, an Indian fellow with a blue turban rushed up to him. "You are Peter Chan?" he said, smiling, showing a mouthful of sparkling gold teeth.

"Yes, I am."

"It is good that I found you so soon," he said in his quaint Indian accent. "Please, I will take your luggage. I am Sammy Sahananden. I will guide you until stated otherwise."

"Are you from Enright?" Peter asked.

"Certainly. Indeed, sir."

Sammy wore khaki slacks and a brightly coloured shirt. His blue turban gave him an air of distinction. "We have a car waiting for you, sir. We shall proceed to the Raffles hotel, for now."

The bright colours of Singapore amazed Peter. At night the scenery had a breathtaking beauty driven by the force of millions of lights draped from pole to pole and along storefronts. Under the powerful streetlights the gaily dressed people appeared very tropical. The Raffles hotel is a large old colonial building at the ocean end of Bras Basah Road. Peter quickly booked into his reserved room. To him, the hotel felt new and profoundly different to what he'd been used to in America. The inner walls being topped with an ornate grill allowed sound and air to circulate freely. In the middle of the ceiling some twelve feet high hung a huge slow turning fan.

The ambience, sound, and smell were strikingly unlike the USA. The bed though very comfortable felt alien and unnatural. After such a long journey, every muscle in his body ached and a good sleep beckoned him with open arms. Sammy made all the necessary arrangements and promised to collect Peter first thing in the morning.

At breakfast the efficient, white-coated staff presented an English style morning feast of tea, toast with marmalade and an ample helping of eggs, bacon, and beans. The entire staff spoke excellent English, making Peter feel welcome and at home.

Sammy arrived almost unperceived. He slipped into the

seat facing Peter. "Good morning, sir. You slept well, I am hoping?"

"Yes, thank you. When do I get to see my new workplace?"

"Mr. Enright wishes you to settle comfortably before you start work. Today we shall visit the head office in Alexandra. For the rest of the week we shall relax and learn to live in Singapore, Singapore very good place."

"I think I'll like it here. The people seem very nice and pleasant."

"You will love Singapore. I shall show you the whole city. It is very good for tourists. Now you finish breakfast, then we go to Alexandra."

A limousine met Peter and Sammy at the front door. The sun shone in a cloudless sky pushing the temperature up into the upper nineties, around 35 Celsius, and the humidity was close to the 100, making it useless to sweat. Much to Peter's relief the limousine had air-conditioning. Sammy, of course, was used to the tropical conditions. The sweltering weather appeared to have no effect on him.

"I'd love a ride on that," Peter said pointing to a three-wheeled bicycle like device with passengers.

"That is trishaw. American sometimes say, rickshaw. Many, many trishaw in Singapore, good for tourist. Very good way to see sights of city," Sammy said with a friendly smile.

The drive to the Enright office tower took about eighteen minutes. The twenty-story modern building stood a little beyond the high-rise residential area, in its own beautiful grounds. Smartly dressed guards at the gate added a military aspect to scene.

"Looks like an armed camp," Peter said.

"Not so. There are no guns," Sammy said adamantly.

The limousine stopped at the canopied main entrance. Inside the glass fronted office tower Peter felt the science fiction-like abidance. Somehow the place seemed to be watching his every move.

A large desk in the foyer, surmounted by a dozen or so

TV monitors, kept tabs on the entire building, inside and out. Sammy led the way to the lift.

"Good morning, Mr. Sahananden," a pleasant female voice said. Sammy pressed his thumb on the lift button and did not reply.

The lift car arrived and the door opened. "One extra to enter," Sammy said.

"Proceed, Mr. Sahananden and guest," came the voice again.

Sammy led the way into the lift. Peter followed close on his heels. Mr. Enright's office, the largest in the building, had a huge, elegant foyer on the third floor. Several desks were scattered about the spacious room in almost a haphazard manner. Sammy walked to one of the desks and spoke with a beautiful young Eurasian woman. She stood and smiled at Peter. Her long black-glistening hair gave her a look of elegance. The sarong accentuated her curves.

"Please come this way," she said in a pleasant and friendly voice.

Peter followed her through a huge oak door into a very luxurious office just beyond her desk. The office presented an air of opulent modernism, with thick wall-to-wall carpeting and large, probably original, paintings on the walls. At one end, an entire glass wall gave a view of the ocean. A middle-aged Caucasian man sat at the gigantic antique wooden desk with an enormous grin on his face.

"Mr. Chan," the attractive lady said. She turned and left the room, closing the great door behind her.

The chubby little man stood. He ran his hand over his bald pate as if brushing his hair back. "Greetings," he said almost excitedly. Quickly, he manoeuvred around the gigantic desk and grabbed Peter's right hand in both of his. He shook it vigorously. "Welcome aboard, son. Welcome aboard."

"Thank you, sir."

The little man hurried back to his oversized chair on the other side of the desk. "Sit, sit, make yourself comfortable. We don't stand on ceremony here."

Peter nervously fidgeted with the keys in his pocket, slightly overwhelmed by the new surroundings. He felt a little uncomfortable in this man's presence. "Thank you," he said softly.

"You can't begin to know how pleased I am that you decided to join us. You're our first Nobel science prizewinner on staff. You'll have your own lab, your own workers, and your own rules. This company is one big happy family. How was your journey?"

"Okay, I guess," Peter said.

"I'm sorry if all this seems overwhelming, but you are really a great prize for us. We shall have many happy and profitable years together. I'm sure you'll love Singapore. It's a beautiful country if you can afford air-conditioning. And you can." He brushed his bald forehead again. "How are you getting along with Sammy?"

"Very well, thank you."

"Sammy is a good man. He's been with me for twenty years. He has three beautiful daughters, all of whom work for me. We operate under seven different company names in twelve different countries. But this is the heart, the dynamic centre, where the puppeteer pulls all the strings, you could say."

"Your lab is a top security place out at Changi. You'll like Changi; beautiful clean beaches, very nice district, well out of the city. Sammy will help you find a house. When you get settled, you can bring your lovely fiancée over."

"Thank you, sir."

"It'll take a while to get settled in. Don't worry, there's plenty of time. You're young. What? Only thirty-four?"

"Yes, sir."

"Here, we work better if we are relaxed. Do you golf at all?"

"Some. Not very well though."

"There's a charming golf course at Seletar. Sammy will sort that out for you too. Now take this." He handed Peter a small bracelet.

"Thank you, sir. What is it?"

The little man sighed very loudly. "I'm sorry. I get carried away with my own enthusiasm. I am Enright. I own everything, though I don't run everything. People who are qualified are paid to do what is required for me. This bracelet was my idea. I was afraid of losing my daughter after her mother died, you see."

"I see," Peter said, lying and feeling a little confused.

"Wear the bracelet either on your wrist or your ankle. It's an isotopic excitable reflector. It can be scanned from up to fifty miles away, and having a very low reflectoflourescity, it will return an encoded echo. The transmitter receiver can decode the reflection, thus identifying the wearer."

"Is that how the elevator works? Oh, I guess you call it a lift."

"Very smart indeed. You already noticed it in use. Your finger scans will be fed into the computer so that with any button you press, the auto security will know if you are who you say you are. It's a great security device, also helps us record where our people are at all times. The computer knows when and where you are at work. A sort of big brother is watching you."

"The one I gave my daughter is slightly different. It's a pendant. If she gets lost or is abducted, the pendant will give her position away. Our security forces would soon bring the deviants to justice."

"Very clever," Peter said.

"There are so many bad people in this world, a little girl just isn't safe, you know."

"I guess you're right."

"Of course, door scanners are very low power. We do have one long-range search scanner. It's the one we used for testing the system. Did you know that the isotope can give one thousand million combinations? That's almost enough to give half the people in the world one."

"Yes, very good," Peter said partially confused. "Do I have to wear it. I mean, is it compulsory?"

"Oh no. If you wish, you may carry it in your pocket. If you don't have it, you'll have difficulty getting around in any of our facilities, could even get arrested," he said and laughed.

"Oh, that's okay, I just don't wear jewellery. When do I start work?"

The chubby man laughed again. "Don't be in such a hurry. Sammy will help you get settled in. He's one of our best security men. He's yours. Why not think about starting sometime next week? You're of Asian descent – have you been to Singapore before?"

"No. My mother was Vietnamese and my father was an American serviceman. I was only a small kid when Saigon fell, so you see, I was educated in the United States."

"Well, you'll be at home here. Singapore is a country of multiple cultures. It's the most cosmopolitan city in the world. Enjoy yourself, take it easy, this is the tropics."

"Yes, sir. Thank you, sir."

"My daughter will be coming over here for her school holidays. Since her mother died, she's all I've got. I'm taking three weeks off to give her a good time." He stood up. "You probably won't see me for a month. Think of yourself as the boss of our Changi research branch, and Sammy is your right-hand man." He stuck out his hand again. "Welcome aboard, son." He smiled.

Peter shook the man's hand. "Thank you, sir. I'm sure we'll get along famously."

As though on cue, the pretty Eurasian girl opened the huge oak door, entered and smiled sweetly. It was obvious that the interview with the big cheese was at an end. Peter silently followed the woman out of the office. Sammy sat by the woman's desk waiting, his bright eyes highlighted by his powerful grin. "So, now you are one of us."

"Yup."

"It is time that you enjoy life. I will take you places, places you have never seen before."

The heat was an overwhelming ninety-eight degrees 'F' and ninety percent humidity. Perspiration streamed down Peter's face, his chest and back soaked. "It's far too hot to enjoy life here.

I had no idea it would be this hot. Is this normal?"

"You will soon get used to it – you must drink plenty water. I would like to take you to Tiger Balm Gardens. The gardens of Haw Par Villa."

"I don't think so, Sammy. I'd like to start work as soon as I can, especially if the plant is air-conditioned."

Sammy laughed. "Work can wait. We shall enjoy the day. Let us be like the tourists while we can. Please, you come to Tiger Balm with Sammy, we enjoy the day."

"Alright, you win. I'll go with you. Let's see this place to you're talking about."

"Excellent, sir. You will enjoy. Everyone enjoy Tiger Balm Gardens."

In only fifteen minutes, the limousine pulled to a halt at the gate of the pleasure park. The two men climbed out and headed up the slope toward the ticket kiosk. Peter was suitably impressed by the surroundings. The entrance looked like a Chinese pagoda with its typically Asian colours and form.

"Well, what is this place?" Peter said, looking around in amazement.

"Most unusual. It is where you will find all the Chinese folklore and beliefs, made in the concrete."

Definitely different from anything Peter had seen before, he stood, trying to absorb the wonder and beauty. The tales of folklore recreated and modelled in cement, people, and monsters from nightmares, dreams, and stories. Some models are life-sized, while some are petite. Even a few of the trees and birds are hand-made. Almost all the magnificent displays were outdoors and in the tropical sun.

Unexpectedly, Peter found himself alone. Sammy had vanished into the milling spectators. About fifteen minutes had passed when another Indian gentleman came to Peter and introduced himself. "I am Arjit Singh," he said in a deep soothing voice. "I shall complete the tour for you." He wore a white turban and had no gold teeth.

"What happened to Sammy, where is he?"

"Sammy has been called away urgently," Arjit said. "Do not worry yourself. I shall take good care of you until Sammy is able to work again. Please relax."

"Well, what happened?"

"Family trouble. Please do not bother yourself. Sammy will be all right. Where would you like to go now, Mr. Chan?"

"How did you recognize me?"

The new guide grinned, and his eyes flashed with personal pride. "Famous person, like Mr. Chan." He laughed. "Everyone know Mr. Chan. Your picture has been in all the newspapers. Everyone knows you come to Singapore."

"Well," Peter said thoughtfully. "I'd like to go to my lab in Changi or go back to my hotel. This heat is overpoweringly oppressive I need air-conditioning."

"It is no problem, sir. Sammy has taken the car. If you wish we can go by boat. There is one at DesJardin Steps. We can take the sea route to Changi, very nice journey and cool. This will be very nice for you; it is much cooler on the water."

"Well, I hope you're right. Is the water calm?"

"Oh, yes, sir. You will enjoy. Please follow me."

Peter was not thinking clearly and could see no harm in taking the boat trip with a total stranger, after all everyone seemed so kind and thoughtful. They did everything differently in Singapore, and he would rather not insult anyone accidentally. Only a five-minute walk from the gardens, and they were on the edge of the water. A small sampan boat lay tied up at the jetty. There were two other people and the driver waiting in it. The men looked rather shady characters; Peter assumed them to be security agents.

As soon as Peter Chan was aboard, the little outboard engine started. Some people on the shore cast-off, and the journey smoothly began. It was cooler on the sea; the breeze from their forward motion kept the temperature down to almost acceptable levels.

"We will pass close to State House, maybe even see the president having a tea party," Arjit said.

Houses on sticks lined some of the coast and children played at the water's edge. A delightful and enlightening journey at first pleased and calmed Peter. After a while, he noticed that they were moving farther and farther away from the shore. "We seem to be heading out to sea," he said with concern.

"Not to worry, sir. See that ship?" He pointed to a luxury cabin cruiser sitting way off in the distance.

"Yes, I see it."

"It is the six-hundred-ton pleasure yacht, '*Miasaki II*.' A very nice boat operated by your boss. It will take us to Changi. It as air conditioning."

Peter relaxed as the small craft manoeuvred its way to the large diesel-powered luxurious yacht. The calm ocean swelled gently, displaying shimmering deep blue with green patches. The world felt peaceful and pleasant in tranquil waters. In a short time, they pulled alongside the *Miasaki II*. Only the driver remained on the small boat. As soon as they were aboard the big diesel yacht, its main engines started and the boat began moving at a good speed away from Singapore.

"Arjit," Peter said. "Why are we going in this direction? Singapore's that way."

"Do not worry yourself. Come, I will take you to see the captain." Arjit led the way to the rear deck.

The aft deck was canopied and open on all sides except the front. The furniture though upholstered in waterproof fabric looked elegant. A fat Chinese-looking man sat on one of the easy chairs. Two good-looking young women stood awaiting his every command. The scene appeared to Peter as a page from a cheap Victorian novel. The Chinese overlord sat with his long cigarette holder dangling from his clawlike hands and the pretty scantily dressed girls standing merely as decorations.

Peter was led before the small group and ordered to sit.

"I am very pleased to see you, Mister Chan," the fat man said softly, and in excellent English. "My name is Chow Peng. You are going to work for me." He knocked a long ash from the end of his cigarette, as though it were a significant act.

Peter's eyes widened with surprise. "I am?"

The fat man tossed a small plastic cube to an armed guard, standing close by. With a meaningful nod of his head, he indicated his intentions. The guard stepped toward Peter and handed him the small block.

Turning the thing in one hand, Peter eyed the four-inch grey cube with interest. "So what is it?"

"This is why you are here, Mr. Chan."

"What exactly is it and why exactly am I here?"

"It's the heart of the dragon, Mr. Chan. You will be the one who will tell me exactly what it is."

"I don't understand. I came to Singapore to work for Enright Enterprises. I was engaged personally by Mr. Enright. I don't know you."

The fat man laughed so mush that his bulk wobbled like a jelly. "Let me demonstrate what I mean when I say you will work for me." He turned to face a guard standing by the entrance and angrily shouted something in a dialect of Chinese.

Things began to happen fast. Two Asian guards arrived carrying submachine guns and stood either side of him. Suddenly, Sammy appeared. He was restrained by one man either side of him.

"Sammy," Peter gasped in surprise. "What are you doing here? What's going on?"

"Silence," the fat man barked, "Mr. Chan, you are my prisoner. You will do as I say, when I say." He turned to one of the guards. "Throw the dog over the side."

"No," Peter yelled, leaping to his feet. Roughly, the two nearest guards arrested his movement.

The other two men forced Sammy to the gunwale and threw him over the side of the boat. "Stop," Peter shouted, struggling with his guards.

"Sit down and shut up," the fat man shouted.

At that moment, gunfire broke out. The guards were shooting at Sammy in the water. Two or three more guards from the front deck joined in shooting as if it were merely an everyday sport.

"Now," Chow Peng said when the gunfire ceased. "You see that I do not joke. I am the lord and master on this vessel. Your life is in my hands, Mr. Chan. Do not doubt that I will use any means to obtain the ends I desire."

"I've been kidnapped," Peter said in amazement.

ISLAND 703

Chapter 2

Suddenly, thunder rattled the glass in the boat's windows as if God himself were angry. The yacht heaved violently and the lightening illuminated the cabin in frightening trades of light. Peter clung to his bunk, wondering if they would flounder in this sudden pestilence. Two armed guards burst into the room. "You," said one. "Out."

Without answering, Peter climbed from his bunk and obeyed the man's gesticulations. 'Perhaps the boat was sinking,' he thought, and it was time to abandon ship.

He was quickly hustled to Chow Peng's office. The guards remained in the room, one either side of the only door. "Now what?" Peter growled, trying to keep his balance in the violent weather.

Chow Peng smiled a greasy smile. "We will not harm you for you are here to help us solve a small riddle. Take a seat and relax, Mr. Chan."

"Relax, how can I relax in this weather?"

"Take a seat. This minor storm is only a Sumatra and will pass as quickly as it arrived."

Peter sat and felt no comfort in the China-man's words. "Why am I here?"

"I am being paid, let us say, by a foreign power to solve a

mystery. Please, sit quietly and listen to what I have to say."

"I don't care," Peter said angrily. "Take me back to Singapore. Take me back right now."

"Mr. Chan, I think you are missing the whole point. You have no say in this matter. You are here to solve a mystery. Failing to do so will mean your death. We have eleven other scientists working on the problem. It was felt, that with your background you would be the only man in the world who could solve it. This cube is part of a great mystery." The fat man leaned forward and handed the cube to Peter.

The abrupt storm was already abating. The thunder had stopped, and the ocean slowly returned to tranquility. The China-man was right about its short duration. Almost reluctantly, Peter raised the cube to the light, looking through it. "What is it?" he asked.

"That is the question, Mr. Chan. You are the genius; you became a Ph.D. at only twenty-eight tender years. You are the expert. It is now your task to decipher this device. Twenty-two people have died investigating that thing, and I am reaching the limit of my patience. We must have an answer soon. Very soon. You will remain my prisoner until we have that answer. We could apprehend your young lady as easily as we did you. I am sure you do not want anything unfortunate to happen to her, now do you?"

Peter responded by tossing the cube onto Chow Peng's desk. "I don't like being threatened. I work my best when I work for the ends I understand. Where did you get that cube, and why did you pick on me?"

He wanted nothing to do with this obviously criminal affair, yet he was curious. There was, however, no real choice. With only a single word from Chow Peng, the two guards grabbed Peter roughly and dragged him back to his cabin. They threw him inside and locked the door.

It was some time later when the guards returned. They opened the door and indicated to Peter that he should follow them once again. He was led to the cabin that served as the overlord's office. The fat Mr. Chow Peng sat behind the large desk. "Come in and sit," he said in a warm, almost friendly tone of voice.

Peter sat, and the two guards stayed inside by the door. "You won't get away with this, you know," Peter said softly. "They will be looking for me."

Chow Peng laughed. "No one is looking for you, and even if they were, they wouldn't find you. Put the thoughts of escape or rescue right out of your head, it will not happen. Please settle down to help. Enjoy life with us. This is why you are here," he said, producing another cube from his desk drawer.

"So what is it?" Peter said emphatically. "Where are you getting these cubes?"

"As I told you before, it is the heart of the dragon. You will have to find out how it works and why it works."

"I don't understand, what is it for?"

Chow Peng smiled. "You must find that out for us too. Let me tell you a short story."

"Sure, I'm not going anywhere, am I?"

"During World War Two, a detachment of twelve Japanese soldiers were put ashore on Island 703."

"Where's that?" Peter said.

"Do not interrupt, Mr. Chan. Just listen, and you will learn. The Japanese soldiers were there to watch and report on American activities. In the confusion of war, the platoon became lost. All but one died. Corporal Miasaki was the only survivor. He stayed at his post until delirium overtook him in 1957. The war had been over for twelve years."

"A certain Mr. Yashimoto, an American-born Japanese playboy, sailed his luxury yacht into a natural harbour at the secluded and uninhabited Dragon's Nest Island. Moments after the anchor dropped, a madman came rushing down the beach, firing at them with his rifle. At the water's edge, he collapsed and fell to the sand."

"Mr. Yashimoto sent men ashore to investigate this unexpected event. It transpired that the madman was Corporal

Miasaki, the lone survivor of Island 703. He was taken aboard the luxury yacht and administered to. They gave him food, water, and medical attention. The raggedy little Japanese soldier had no idea that the war had ended many years prior. He told a strange and wonderful tale that Yashimoto recorded on audio tape."

Peter sighed. "I would rather not hear this tale. When does it become relevant to the cube? Let's get to the point, shall we?"

"My dear, Mr. Chan, how do you expect to understand without listening?"

"Very well, go on get on with it."

"Corporal Miasaki died soon after he was admitted to hospital in Tokyo. The tape recording of his adventures remained the property of Mr. Yashimoto. No one saw the significance of the recording until the day I heard it. Mr. Yashimoto and his empty-headed friends would listen to the tape at cocktail parties, as if it were some silly party favour."

"When I heard the story, I knew it to be real. Listen, I shall play the tape for you." He leaned over and pressed the start button on a cassette recorder.

The tape began to play. The shaky and frail voice of what sounded like an old man began speaking in Japanese. After a few moments, Peter said: "I don't understand Japanese. There is no point in me listening to it, I don't understand a word."

Chow Peng smiled and switched the voice off. "Forgive me. I speak eight Asian dialects, English, and Dutch. Let me play an edited translation for you." He popped the tape out and replaced it with one he removed from his desk drawer.

"The story of Corporal Miasaki," the tape said. "We were twelve in all as we left the submarine and paddled our way to Island 703. We did not know if there were any American or Australian observers already on the island. Full precautions had to be observed until we had established the island to be ours."

"So what?" Peter said. "I believe you; we don't have to go through all this, just tell me in a few words what happened."

"Please listen to the tape," Chow Peng snapped angrily.

The tape continued, "The island was not occupied by any human foe, but instead by a deadly, unrelenting dragon. A great central lava flow lay like a road down from the central peak almost to the beach. At the end of the flow lay a pool of clear sweet water that welled up from beneath the ground. The pool area made a good place to camp. The ancient volcanic flow gave quick access to the high ground."

"Four men were sent to circle the island, five to explore the high ground and three remained to make camp. All went well, we completely explored the island within three days. Our troubles began the day an American airplane came to Island 703. We heard the plane's engines and ran for cover. As I watched the enemy aircraft come straight toward us, suddenly lightning leapt from the mountain peak and completely destroyed the machine."

"It was truly a bad omen. Soon after the attack, we all clearly heard the dragon breathing deep in the ground. That night, one of the men noticed that there was a light visible in the limpid pool. If you knelt down to drink from the pool, as your face touched the water, the light became visible."

Peter leaned forward and shut the tape machine off. "Now I understand. You set me up – the man on the plane and everything. You set this whole thing up to bring me out here, and for this, a science fiction tale."

Chow Peng smiled. "Do you not find the story interesting, Mr. Chan?"

"It's the Banda Sea Triangle, isn't it? You planned it all from the start. That man on the plane, and the magazine article the whole ball of wax."

"I wanted your mind primed with curiosity."

"What about Enright? Is he just another employee of yours? Or will they try to follow me?"

"Alas," Chow Peng sighed. "You're lost at sea; dead I suspect. They may find that Indian's body, but they will think the sea swallowed you. Now may we listen to the rest of the tape?"

"Sure, I guess so."

The fat China-man leaned forward and pressed the button.

"Two men stripped and entered the cold water," continued the tape machine. "They swam down into the limpid pool. Soon they disappeared. They were never seen again, but the dragon could be heard consuming them. It was a most terrible sound. We could not leave the island, nor could we make radio contact. Something caused severe radio interference. We would have to wait for a passing ship."

"As time passed, the dragon became louder and louder. At first, we had to put an ear to the ground to hear him, but as time passed, he could be heard almost at any time. It would take a deep breath, and then slowly, wheezing, would breathe out. The sound was terrible and frightening. His pulse could at times also be heard."

"One day, Turboki came running down the long lava flow yelling that he had found a cave. I took five men, including Turboki. We marched bravely up the long slope to where the flow started. Turboki jumped off the edge descending some five feet to a small plateau. There he pointed out a hole in the cliff face, almost hidden by undergrowth."

"Turboki disappeared into the hole. We all followed, myself last. I could hear them talking ahead of me. Hand lanterns were used to light our way inside the passage. At the very end, the passage narrowed, so small that the only way in, was to lie down and wriggle through. As I put my head into the hole, I could see we had found some kind of room. The tunnel exit was two or three feet from the floor."

"At the far end of the room stood a door with no handle. Near it and on the wall, a shiny button beckoned the curious. As I was about to wriggle through the hole, Turboki put his hand on the shining button. It awakened the awful dragon and it roared. With a sound like thunder, the room became filled with white dancing fire. All five of my men were consumed. Terrified and almost choking on the dreadful fumes and smell of burned flesh, I wriggled back and fled from the cave."

"Again, the dragon had tasted human flesh. For a while,

his breathing could be heard all over the island. His strength grew with every feeding. We feared that soon he would be strong enough to leave his hiding place and roam the land freely consuming and destroying without hindrance. A rifle offered no defence against such supernatural powers."

"The weeks turned to months, the months to years, and two more men died of fever. We stayed away from the dragon. He became peaceful. Even his breathing could barely be heard. Never did our countrymen come for us. We saw not even a friendly ship upon the sea. Three of us marched up and down, pretending not to notice the years slipping by."

"One day, when I returned to camp from watch on a high point of the island, I found Noguchi dead. He had been stabbed to death with a bayonet. Comarra was missing. It was obvious that they had been fighting. Comarra was never seen again. The loneliness of the island and the constant heartbeat of the dragon slowly sends a man to madness."

"I lost count of the days. There seemed no point in watching. No one had visited 703 in years, why should they now? I wandered the island searching for anything edible. There are no animals and very few birds. The dragon either consumed them or frightened them away. A terrible and strange thing happened to me on one of these wanderings."

"One early morning, long before the sun reached its height. I walked up the lava flow toward the pinnacle. At the cliff's end, I turned left and made my way along a ledge and so to a sloping plateau. While searching the edge of the plateau, I slipped and fell. When I awoke, the sun had reached its zenith, and my head was bleeding. I felt feeble and knew that the end would soon come. My rifle was nowhere to be found."

Peter again turned off the tape recorder. "I've heard enough of this drivel. Take me back to Singapore, and no more will be said of the matter."

"My dear, Mr. Chan, relax, sit back and listen. We are yet to hear the most exciting part of the story."

"I would rather not listen to a madman. The poor guy was

delirious and overly superstitious. There could be no dragon. They don't exist, surely you must know that."

"Listen and learn, Mr. Chan. Corporal Miasaki died giving us a perfect opportunity." He leaned forward and started the tape once more.

"Suddenly, I saw a hole in the side of the cliff face. Remembering what happened to my men the last time, I thought that it would be a quick and honourable way to die. Barely able to fit, I wriggled into the vent. Unlike the first time, there was no light though it did lead to a mysterious room. The chamber was barren and totally dark. I could hear a soft hum – the sound of delicate machinery running. There was also a smell of clean and refreshing coolness."

"Slowly, I felt my way along the wall and found a corridor with dim light at the far end. Taking all my courage, I walked to the lighted end. I found the passage to be a very thin corridor. On the wall barring the way to a large, illuminated room stood a screened air vent. Looking through the grill, I could see that there were ten coffins in the chamber. At least two were occupied."

"Carefully, I removed the grill and lowered myself into the mortuary. This had to be the dragon's larder a place where he kept his reserve supply of food. The coffins were storage devices. A dead man lay in each of two coffins, but all the other bodies must have been eaten already. Everything was cold. Ice clung to the walls like the inside of a butcher's meat store. My breath steamed as I breathed. There was only one exit, and it was closed."

"Unlike the other place, there were no buttons to press. Timidly, I pushed the door. It yielded to my touch, revealing yet another door. As I approached the second, the first one closed by itself. The spirit of the dragon moved it. The second door opened at a push, which revealed a long corridor with entrances on both sides. Again, unseen lanterns lighted the hall-like passage. The ceiling almost as bright as the daylight sun, casting light everywhere and with no shadows."

"As if in a trance, I walked to the only door open to me. I saw a room of great mysticism. I cannot describe the interior, for everything therein is beyond my reason. The only familiar thing I saw was a chair, a chair of great complexity – a throne, perhaps. It could only be the chamber of the lord of the dragon. A soft, pleasant voice spoke to me in a foreign tongue. In fear, I kneeled and began to pray for forgiveness. I did not want the wrath of the dragon unleashed upon me."

"In a short time, the voice told me to sit on the throne. It spoke in my own language. Though filled with fear beyond any I have ever experienced, I obeyed the hidden master. As soon as I sat, a miracle occurred. There before me in a glass frame were familiar pictures of my wife and my children. It was a miracle beyond my comprehension. The voice said many things to me in my own tongue."

"It asked if I was of the old ones. I could not know. I answered 'Yes,' as I am old. The voice asked why it did not recognize me. I did not know the answer. It seemed that the voice was angry with me for something that I could not understand. It asked if I had come from the room of ice. My answer was in the affirmative. My experience with the dragon lord of the island became more terrible."

"The voice demanded that I be repaired and ordered that I report to the room of the dragon's claw. In terrible fear, I staggered to the room designated. It was wondrous, and frightening. I stood on the appointed spot and prayed that I may be preserved. The sound of an unholy monster came and with it a terrible spider that walked across the ceiling. The spider was as big as a man."

"Suddenly, the awful claw of the dragon descended. It lifted me and carried me to where the spider burned me. I don't know how long I lingered there, for in fear, I lost consciousness. When I awoke the claw carried me to the spot where I had started. Staggering, I walked back to the room of the terrible oracle. The voice told me that now the dragon would be my friend and would not harm me. I could wander without fear of reprisal."

"The voice had not lied. After that time, I could open any door. At the end of the corridor there were steps that led up one flight. At the top was a door of burnished gold. As I approached, the door vanished into the wall. The room beyond was the temple of the demon. Guardians of solid gold stood either side of the door, their curly and coloured umbilical still attached to their naval. It was a sight to put fear in any man's heart."

"A great door opposite opened and I wandered through and down the steps. I found another room of great miracles at the bottom. The chamber had the likeness of the island in windows. Even the sea could be seen to move. On my way back, I found another door in the room of the golden idols. The door opened and I entered. In there, I found the five skeletons of my comrades who were destroyed by the dragon. I took one of the rifles, as I had lost my own."

"At the bottom of the steps, near the room of the oracle, I found another door. It opened and I entered. A small staircase led in a circle to a floor below. The room was very strange, with water that welled up out of the floor and flowed to the end of the long room. I could hear the dragon breathing, and his heartbeat was clear. At the end of the room where the water dropped through the floor was another entrance."

"The second door opened when I touched the shiny button. This room was like the first. I walked down the steps. At the bottom water welled up through the floor and flowed to the end of the room. The dragon's voice became loud, and the room warm from his breath. I pressed the plate of another door to the side. I dared not enter. The dragon's voice was loud and his heartbeat thunderous. I stepped back and the door closed."

"Many years later, while on the beach, I was taken by the spirit of the island. I knew that I would die, for I had not the strength to go back to the dragon. I lay there for many days when I saw a boat of the American Navy. They were discharging troops to capture my island and conquer my dragon. I called the dragon to help me. Then taking my rifle, I attacked the enemy. I remember no more until I awoke here."

"So," Peter said. "The poor old guy was totally insane. He really believed the dragon to be real. I guess he'd probably read some Jewels Vern or a Japanese equivalent."

"Do you not see the significance of what he experienced?" Chow Peng said in a growling tone of voice.

"Not really. I mean, the guy was obviously delirious for years. Quite likely insane. Loneliness and poor diet gave him hallucinations. And being superstitious, he personified the dragon."

Chow Peng grinned from ear to ear. "The dragon is merely a machine, some form of guardian that attacks aircraft which fly over it yet leaving water vessels alone. The fabled Banda Sea Triangle."

Peter laughed. "You mean you've brought me here to have a look at the Banda Sea Triangle? You must be as crazy as poor old Miasaki."

"For a man of such high intelligence and great learning, you have no imagination. Miasaki found a machine probably built by aliens, maybe hundreds of years ago. Equipment that is some form of guardian that protects something. Something so valuable, the machine kills indiscriminately to protect it. I've been there and seen the place. It is real, terrible, and terrifying. It kills swiftly and unpredictably with a power beyond imagination. Twenty-two of my men have been killed by that monster. It still hides its secrets, and still resists every move I make against it."

"You will learn to understand this exceptional dragon so that we may partake of its many and great secrets. That cube is from the very heart of the dragon, yet no one can understand the workings of it. It remains a mystery, as is life. It is the spirit of the dragon, the life force, the spirit of the demon."

"What do you intend to do with the knowledge of this thing, should you ever get it?"

"Knowledge is power, Mr. Chan, and power is all there is."

"So, what do you intend to do with this power or knowledge?"

"I shall sell the secret to the highest bidder."

Peter breathed out in deep thought. "You are only interested in the money, a mercenary?"

"Money too is power. Your country thinks it rules the world. All accomplished with money, the power of the almighty dollar. Money from the colonies, extorted from the people. America takes what it wants because it has the money to enforce its views."

"I think you've got it all wrong. The States is a free country. A democracy. The people rule not some jumped up dictator. There's no tyranny, no extortion. Have you ever been to the States?"

Chow Peng laughed heartily. His enormous, fat belly heaved and quaked in a sickening manner. "A man as intelligent as you and you believe the propaganda expounded by your corrupt power and money-hungry politicians."

Peter shook his head. "I won't work for you. I can't. You represent chaos and disorder. You are one of the bad guys."

Again, Chow Peng laughed. He laughed until his eyes ran freely with tears. "I hope for all our sakes you can solve this mystery. If you do not, then you will certainly die. I shall see to it personally."

"Threats don't frighten me. Right will always prevail. It's the law of nature – the way of things. The will of the people and all that."

"Not in this particular case, Mr. Chan. Your life is in my hands, until you die or succeed. Or perhaps do both."

"Enright will figure out where we are going. He has both money and power. He'll hound you to the ends of the earth."

"I think not. The rest of your journey will be under the sea. Besides, who, in their right mind would believe the story of Dragon's Nest Island?"

"I would."

THE DEVIL'S KITCHEN

Chapter 3

As the sunlight slowly failed and the sky began taking on a deep red hue, the Miasaki II came to a full stop. She bobbed gently in the light swell, completely beyond the sight of any land. A World War II submarine surfaced only a hundred yards from the luxury yacht. The hatches opened, and Asian sailors climbed onto the submarine's deck.

In minutes, the guards roughly collected Peter and led him to an outboard powered inflated rubber boat. The small dinghy, with Peter, Arjit, and three others, scampered across the short distance to the old submarine whose diesels thundered noisily in the hot summer night. None of the crew spoke a single word of English. Arjit stayed close to Peter and gave him translations of what was being said.

Peter and Arjit were berthed in a single cabin so small, neither could stand up fully. Pipes and wires passed through the tiny room, in one side and out the other. Soon the sound of the diesels stopped and the unmistakable noise of the tanks flooding began. The hum made by the submarine's powerful electric motors seemed more comforting than the diesels.

The next day, when Peter awoke, the sub had surfaced. The diesels rumbled through the whole boat, as it rolled gently on the sea swell. Peter remained constricted in his movements, he was allowed only in the corridor, in the head, and the tiny cabin. Everywhere he went, Arjit stayed close behind. There was little or no contact with the crew just the occasional person passing through the narrow corridors.

The journey to Island 703 seemed to take forever. The confinement, no windows, and bad Chinese food were a combination fit to test the patience of a saint. For six days and five nights, the sub rumbled along on its interminable journey. After the first night, the boat stayed either on or near the surface, allowing the diesel engines to be used all the time.

Suddenly great excitement took the old vessel. Sailors began rushing about, tanks being blown, and a multitude of new and unexplained noises filled the air. Eventually, someone came for Peter and Arjit. They were forbidden to take any possessions with them. The guards led them quickly to the forward deck. The night air put a ghostly, almost unearthly hush on the proceedings. The moon had not risen and the visibility near to zero.

The white navigation light at the top of the conning tower soon attracted a small boat. The tiny vessel with its put-put motor manoeuvred to the submarine's side. Almost in total darkness, aided only by a couple of sailors with flashlights, four people, including Peter and Arjit, climbed into the skiff. Moments later, the small craft departed, leaving the sub to vanish in the darkness. The operator spoke in hushed Chinese to his radio. A light appeared in the distance – the whole affair was most cloak and dagger.

It took five minutes to reach the light. Several people on a small wooden jetty awaited the arrival of the little boat. Pulling alongside, everyone disembarked. The leaders walked with lights pointed toward the ground. Soon they reached a door in the side of a great cliff. It opened, and strong white light streamed out into the tropical night. Everyone hustled quickly into the room beyond, and the door slammed closed. Peter felt like Jonah as it seemed he had been swallowed by a whale.

An officious-looking Chinese gentleman began speaking.

Arjit whispered the translation. "Welcome to Dragon's Nest Island. Here, you are not prisoners. During the day, you may explore the island, but you must complete your work first. Anyone not reporting for their work will be found and shot unquestionably. Please enjoy your stay."

Arjit then spoke to a light-machinegun carrying soldier. He grabbed Peter's hand, and together with the soldier, they walked into one of the many passages, and then to an apartment. There were no windows, just plain straight, walls. The only furniture was two easy chairs, two beds, two cupboards and a large table. The central light had a protective grill around it.

"This is our room," Arjit said with a smile.

"Are you a prisoner, too, or are *you*, my keeper?"

"We are not prisoners in the normal sense. I have work to do and so do you. Together, we shall stay alive."

In the daylight of the following day, Peter was allowed to see the outside of the strange building. The main entrance to the mountain dwelling was covered with a huge camouflage net, hiding it from aerial observation. The door was about twenty feet high and at least thirty feet wide. It looked like rock from the outside. Careful attention had been made to make the entrance invisible to anyone passing the island.

The land sloped down on all sides toward the water from a single peak. There were several small plateaus on the eight-hundred-foot central mountain. All but the highest ground had a dense tree covering. The beach, in most places, was broad, soft, silky sand.

The small door that the people used led into a thirty-by-thirty-foot room beside the great door. What lay beyond the large door would remain a secret for the time being. Late that same afternoon, Peter was taken to a room that had been set up as a laboratory. In there he had to solve the mystery of the cubes, though as yet he hadn't been shown where the cubes came from. Life felt more acceptable in the hollow mountain, and luxurious in comparison to life on the submarine.

Excitement and wonder became the rule for the next day.

Peter and Arjit received a personally guided tour of the known areas. Arjit translated, as the guide spoke no English. Firstly, they visited the area behind the massive door. As the guide explained, Arjit whispered the translation for Peter.

"The black area in the ceiling is where the dragon's sting has been eliminated. Hand launched anti-tank missiles were used to silence the device. Nine men were killed before they destroyed it."

Peter looked around the giant room, noticing that there were no clues as to the real purpose of the place, and only a black smudge on the ceiling where the supposed dragon's sting had been located. "What is this room for?"

"That is not known. It is thought that perhaps the builders had some kind of air vehicle in here. Much time has been spent trying to enter by the great door. Though no one has yet discovered how to open it."

At the end of the room stood another huge door. A hole had been burned in it by an acetylene torch. The hole was large enough to act as a small doorway. Beyond the hole yet another room the size of an aircraft hangar. Here too there was black and burned damage to the illuminated ceiling. "More dragon stings?" Peter asked.

"Yes, seven men were killed silencing them."

"I'm almost afraid to ask. But how did all the people get killed?"

"The dragon lashes out with white fire. It goes straight to a man's heart. It only attacks people in the room where the sting is located."

"What's beyond the big doors at the end?" Peter said, and Arjit translated for him.

"It has not been penetrated yet. Work is now in progress on the little door at the side. Tonight it should be opened."

Organization at the island outpost appeared haphazard and undirected. Peter felt unsure of what his job was supposed to be, or which side Arjit represented. He had a great longing to get off the island and go home to America. He no longer cared to see the

Far East. Peter had nothing to do in the lab, and with no TV, or any other pastime, the whole escapade seemed a great waste of time and apparently very dangerous.

That evening, as he lazed on his bunk, sirens suddenly began to sound. Both he and Arjit were summoned by one of the guards. There was much excitement at the site of the great door.

"They have made a hole in the wall," Arjit said. "You are requested to examine what they have found there."

Peter and Arjit were led to the place where the breach had been made. There were many guards, all wearing flak jackets, helmets, and goggles. Most of them carried small RPG missiles at the ready. The hole in the wall was minimal, about a yard square. Peter's heart pounded with excitement as he approached the place. Someone pointed to the hole and babbled something in Chinese.

Arjit took Peter's hand. "My friend, this is a matter of life and death. Do not put your hands into that hole. The dragon will certainly destroy you if you do. Look and look only, do not attempt to enter."

Pete knelt down at the hole and peeked inside. A picturesque and tiny fairyland presented itself. Many of the strange cubes were glowing, in rows and columns. One stack of cubes appeared brighter than the others and had flickering, running lights inside. The purpose of the devices was far from obvious. Overcome by their beauty, he forgot the warnings. Putting his hand in, he touched one of the cubes. Instantly, it went dark. With a click and a rumble of motors, the great door began opening.

Panic exploded among the onlookers as though a swarm of bees had been released among them. People ran in all directions. Arjit grabbed Peter and wrenched him from the hole. Suddenly, a lightning storm erupted. Fire rained down from the centre of the newly exposed chamber. Some guards returned the fire with missiles. The ear-splitting noise accompanied by enormous flashes and bangs resounding through the halls, deafening all present.

Pete and Arjit lay on the floor just out of the sting's range, playing dead in the hope that the dragon would leave them alone. Soon peace and silence returned to the complex, the battle had, for the moment, come to an end. The room was filled with smoke and the smell of cordite and burned flesh.

"Can we move?" Peter whispered.

"Yes," replied Arjit. "I think it is all over."

The mountain's air-conditioning quickly removed the smoke. Several bodies lay scattered around the floor. Five men had been killed and eleven injured. Peter's heart pounded fit to burst. The excitement and emotion reminded him of the time he and his mother escaped from Saigon. "What happened?" he gasped, feeling as though he wanted to burst into tears.

"It is the dragon's revenge. Nothing must be disturbed, or you will unleash the fury of the dragon. You should have been killed, but instead it opened the door and tried to kill everyone else. You are most fortunate, my friend."

The cubes had become silent and black. There were no longer lights inside them. Pete found that he could remove any cube simply by picking it up. The fury and the fire had ended for the moment. The new room revealed nothing interesting, just a great empty place. There was, however, a small door that had not opened. "That is the way to go," Peter said authoritatively. "Open that small door."

"How can you know this?" Arjit asked.

"Don't know. It's just a feeling. I'm sure that's the way to go. It has to be."

Arjit told the work commander, and the preparations began again for the next leg of the assault on the mountain. Peter Chan took the loose cubes to the lab, where he conducted experiments on them. The Asian explorers accepted him as an expert because he had become the first to remove cubes and live. His advice would be followed in the future.

The workmen began the procedure to open the small door. Acetylene torches were ineffective against its resilient metal. Even a thermal lance had great difficulty cutting through the hinges and the bolt, and then the door would not yield. Piece by piece they hacked away at the reluctant portal, as the hours dragged slowly by.

As the work lingered into the night, Peter lay on his bunk and became sorrowful and melancholy. He thought of all the life he was missing in the outside free world.

"You are looking sad, my friend," Arjit said in his distinctive Indo-English accent.

"I am, and afraid. I don't want to be here in this awful place. I want to go home. I want to go home to America; I've seen enough of Asia to last me a lifetime."

"You may as well enjoy what you have here. It could well be the last thing that you have on this Earth," Arjit said seriously.

"I can't enjoy my work here. It goes against my conscience. I don't believe in slavery and I certainly don't trust that Chinaman who brought us here."

"It is, my friend, better than living in hell."

"What do you know of hell? When I was a kid, I lived in Vietnam. That was hell on earth. Compared to that, this place is heaven."

"I am sorry for you, my friend. But that is in the past. This is the present."

"My dad was almost blown to bits by a land mine. Mother and I dragged him to the American lines. We were evacuated to a ship in the harbour. I'll never forget the terror and the horror. There were dead people laying everywhere, blown apart by indiscriminate artillery – they lay everywhere. The yelling and screaming, the smoke and the smell will stay with me all my life. These people are the same enemy. Why on Earth do you think they want this Dragon tamed?"

"I do not know."

"Subjugation, power, it's just brinkmanship. The USA had the bomb, so these people want whatever powers and guards this island."

Arjit laughed. "Even so my friend, what use is a conscience when you are already in this particular hell?"

"I can't stand it much longer," Peter said. "Work here goes against my principles."

"What principles could be more important than life?"

"The people who brought me here are corrupt. I can't work for them. They abducted me and killed my friend."

"They will kill you if you are of no use to them. You must be useful or you die."

"I can't work for evil."

Arjit smiled. "What is evil? What is good? Even the atomic bomb became good. It supplies heat and light for people. Who are you to judge what is evil?"

"The people who brought us here are not the good guys."

"Maybe, and maybe not. What of this place? Is the dragon good or bad? Are you on the side of the dragon or the dragon slayers?"

Peter thought for a few seconds. "Two evils do not make one good. Helping the slayers is not good if their intent is evil. It doesn't matter whether the dragon is good or bad, they wish to exploit it. The exploitation is the harmful element."

Laughingly, Arjit said, "My friend, I shall do my best to protect you. I think that God brought us both here for some meaningful reason of his own. I think my purpose in this life is to help to protect you. Furthermore, I am not sure what your purpose is, but God would not have brought you here for nothing – everything has a reason and a purpose."

"I wish I had your faith, Arjit, but I'm a coward. I'm afraid of you, and of the people who brought us here. I'm terrified of the dragon. I can't even begin to understand what or who built this place. Its technology is totally beyond my understanding. I feel dwarfed by its intellect and the sheer genius of the builders of this place."

"It is, perhaps," Arjit whispered, "imperative to hurry this experiment. The dragon may have already sent for its masters. They may be on their way even now. God only knows what they will do to us when they find us in the devil's kitchen."

"Oh God! That's not what I want to hear. Why do you help

these people? Let's escape, get the hell out of here together."

Arjit laughed. "I cannot leave. Like you, terrible things will happen to the ones I love. I would like to defeat the slavers and leave here a free man, but that is unrealistic. God has brought me here to complete his purpose and his purpose must be good. God knows everything, even the builders of this place. All will work out the way the Good Lord God has planned it. Evil will become good. Whether we shall see the result here, or be reborn for our troubles, it is unimportant."

Peter calmed down a little, Arjit was right, there was nothing to be done except what they were ordered to do. Outside, the complex was just a jungle island in the middle of a tropical ocean. Miasaki was eventually rescued, but he wasn't chased by rocket and machine gun-toting soldiers.

Tears trickled from the corners of Peter's eyes. "I'm a scientist, not a soldier. I'm a coward. I fear for my life. I can't sleep for all the pressure here. I feel sure, I'll go insane under these conditions."

"Do not fear, my young friend. I believe your purpose here is essential. God has brought me here to look after you. I shall protect you with my life. Take heart, we will escape from this place, and we shall both be much smarter people than before."

"I can't help thinking of Sammy, how easy it was for them to kill him. They'd kill us just as easily."

"Do not speak to them. Speak only to me. I will translate. This will make me valuable to them, and you are the world's leading expert on the cubes."

"I don't know anything about the cubes. They are a total mystery to me."

"Peter, my friend, do not tell them that. Always pretend you know more than you do. They think you are a genius because you were not killed when you took those cubes."

"My ears are still ringing from the rockets they fired. Can't we stop them doing that? It's pure insanity."

"No," Arjit said firmly.

Suddenly, a siren sounded. "Now what?" Peter said jumping

to his feet.

"It means they have cut through another door, and they will come for you in a moment."

Just as Arjit finished speaking, a loud banging came to their door. He opened it and two armed guards stood awaiting them. For several seconds they conversed, voices raised. One guard struck Arjit on the chest with the butt of his weapon. Still in pain and holding his chest he turned to Peter. "They want you to enter the place they have opened. I shall come with you."

Roughly the two were led to the newly made entrance near the giant door. It had been crudely burned from its mounts. The orifice beyond was dark and uninviting. The chief yelled something.

"You have to enter," Arjit whispered. "Or they will shoot you where you stand."

Trembling from head to foot, Peter replied, "Great choice, death by lightning or death by firing squad." slowly he advanced toward the gaping breach. Some light fell through the hole and showed dimly that there were stairs beyond the door. Breathing heavily, he passed through the opening. With eyes closed he waited for the thunder and lightning, cringing at every tiny sound.

"Perhaps the Dragon sleeps," Arjit whispered.

Peter felt his pounding heart was the loudest sound in the entire mountain. "I hope you're right my friend."

Cautiously, the two ascended the dark stairs. Unexpectedly, the lights came on throwing the fear of God into both men. It was nothing more than a spiral staircase. The walls were clean, smooth polymerized rock. The fearful sound of the dragon breathing could clearly be heard. A heavy metallic door barred the way at the top of the stairs.

In only a few moments, the missile carriers and other soldiers cautiously climbed the steps. The situation became rather crowded. Peter and Arjit wrestled their way down back to the larger room at the bottom. The soldiers were jubilant it was the first area penetrated without men dying. Like ants, they continued their tasks. Lugging heavy machinery up the steps to assail the next door.

That night, Peter lay on his bunk, his mind whirling with confusing thoughts. Nothing he had seen made any sense. The Dragon was a mystery which would probably remain that way. Why the mountain did or at times did not retaliate was also a mystery. The bright and beautiful cubes that died of their own accord and changed their form was yet another puzzle.

If the mountain wanted to kill them, why did it provide air, coolness and electrical power? The entire place was an enigma and a contradiction unto itself.

INTRUDER ALERT

Chapter 4

There were no windows in the mountain bastion. Only a clock separated night from day. Studying the cubes in his new lab, Peter began to understand how they worked. Pulses that radiated through the air like radio waves caused the cubes to reorganize their internal structure. The inner structural organization gave the cube its purpose, which was dictated by an unseen source.

The code that caused the appropriate organization of the cube's inner material remained elusive. Peter could cause a cube to change, yet he could not get it to do anything useful. How multiple cubes simultaneously communicated was as yet a conundrum. Something in the mountain radiated a form of communication and cleverly talked only to the cubes it wanted or needed to converse with.

Peter lay on his bed. His thoughts drifting to those who he loved and missed, and to the employment that would have been his if he had not been abducted. Because of Arjit's lectures, he felt that there was no way to leave the island alive. His captors would kill him when his purpose concluded. He looked at Arjit, who lay face up, sleeping quietly. "I think you're doomed too, my helpful friend."

The alarm sounded, yet another door penetrated. Arjit sat

up. "I suppose we are in business again," he said sleepily.

A banging came to their door. Peter and Arjit rose and walked to the exit. Sure enough the guards were there, demanding that Peter risk his life in another opened section.

The door at the top of the newly exposed spiral staircase had a hole burned through it, large enough for a man to pass. One of the armed Chinese struck Peter with his weapon and indicated the hole. The obvious intention was for him to enter it. Darkness obscured the forbidden interior.

More than trepidation caused Peter's whole body to shake. Every man has a fear of the unknown and here the unknown usually meant death.

"Take care," Arjit said softly. "I shall follow you whether you live or die."

With a pounding heart Peter bent his head down and gingerly pushed forward into the hole. His blood froze with shock as the lights came on. Perspiration trickled down his face and back. His entire body became wet, and his hands trembled uncontrollably.

"Perhaps the Dragon's sting is no more," Arjit said softly. "I, for one, am thankful."

Peter did not answer, he opened his eyes to observe the room he had entered. At the far end of the thirty by ten-foot room, in the centre of the wall, stood another metallic, reinforced locked door. About halfway down the wall on the right yet another door, this time of a different type. The different portal had an illuminated pad on the wall next to it. There were no telltale marks on the ceiling to give any indication of the dragon's sting.

Slowly the soldiers filtered into the room. With weapons at the ready, some soldiers trembled, and all eyes were alert. Each man was ready to flee should the strike begin. The silence felt as overpowering as the noise had been, and still no response from the death-dealing mountain.

"Press the button," Arjit whispered.

Timidly, Peter walked to the closed door – the thought of

old Miasaki foremost in his mind. Would the mountain explode in a cascade of death and destruction if he touched the plate? Gingerly he put his hand to the illuminated panel. Instantly, the door vanished into its frame. The whooshing sound terrified the timid intruders. Most of the soldiers fell to the floor in an attempt to take cover. The newly revealed room was the most amazing discovery yet.

A cold white light illuminated the new chamber, giving it an air of sterility and perfection. The chamber was about twenty-five by twenty-five feet. The walls were smooth and unbroken except for the entry door and one other. A large console occupied the majority of the floor space. A single seat, obviously designed for a human stood at the centre of the desk-like console.

There were no light switches visible, except for another illuminated pad beside the opposite door. Cautiously, Peter crept into the room. He scanned the ceiling for signs of the deadly sting. The ceiling somehow radiated all the light, giving a shadow free environment and not a trace of anything harmful. Quietly, he slid into the only seat, with Arjit close behind him.

The console had three flat screen displays, all in full colour and working. The largest, in the centre of the desk, had a picture of the south end of the island. The other two displayed other parts of the island. Although there were hundreds of buttons on the desk, no one dared touch any of them.

"What is it?" Arjit whispered as though afraid the machine would hear him.

"Some kind of control centre. Though what it controls I haven't the faintest idea."

Slowly and still wary of the Dragon's sting, Peter stood and walked to the second door. He carefully placed the palm of his hand on the lighted pad. Instantly the door slid aside revealing a cubicle, approximately six by six feet. The well-illuminated, small, empty room seemed to serve no particular purpose. Both Peter and Arjit slowly entered, carefully examining the ceiling and walls for signs of the deadly sting.

As Arjit cleared the door, it slid silently closed. Suddenly, the room descended. It stopped and the door opened. It was an elevator that had taken them to the foot of the spiral staircase. As they exited the door closed and once more became hidden from sight.

"A quick exit?" Arjit said. "But how does one use it from this end?"

Peter shook his head. "Just another puzzle. I'd like to do some work on the room with the picture screens."

Arjit laughed. "I am sure you will."

A guard came running down the spiral stairs. He struck Arjit on the chest with the butt of his riffle. Several angry words were exchanged. The guard turned to Peter but did not strike him.

"I swear," Arjit said. "If anyone does that again, I will have to kill them. We must return to the picture room. Our lord and master wish you to demonstrate the use of the elevator."

They made their way back to the control centre with the occasional prod from the guard. There were several people in the room, some in white coats. The chief Chinese man stood close to the elevator entrance. With a wave of his hand, he indicated the luminous panel. Peter pressed it with his palm and the door opened, much to the surprise of the leader.

"Mr. Lie say, close it again," Arjit said.

"I can't do that. I don't know how."

"Mr. Lie say, close it now."

"I can't. Mr. Lie is a fool," Peter said.

The Chinese man stepped forward. "Mr. Lie may be a fool, but Mr. Lie will outlive this project," he said in excellent English.

"You speak English?" Peter said in surprise.

Mr. Lie grinned awkwardly. "I speak five language, ver' good. How many you speak?"

"Well, only one."

"You are world genius? You are American trash. I not like your kind. You are here, you will do as I say, or you will die here."

"I can't close the door. I don't know how to."

Lie walked into the elevator. "Door does not close," he said angrily.

Peter walked in. Immediately, the door closed. Lie and Peter were alone in the descending car. It stopped and the door opened. The two stepped out of the lift. "You see," Peter said. "I didn't do anything."

They walked back to the control room. "Somehow the Dragon recognizes you," Lie said. "You know more than you tell."

"No, I don't. I can't understand why, but, well, I just don't know. Things seem to happen, and I don't have any control over them."

They entered the control room again. Lie walked over to the lighted panel on the wall. He placed his palm on it. The lift door remained closed. "Open it. Open this door."

Peter placed his palm on the plate, instantly the door opened. "I don't understand. Honest, I don't understand why it works for me and not you."

Lie pouted. "I will get the truth from you if I have to remove it by surgery."

"Let me examine this room. Clear out all these white coats. I'm sure I can solve the mystery of this room if you leave it to me."

Lie glanced around the room and then shouted something in another language. The white coats and the soldiers left the room. "You have this thing to yourself. Show me how it works in twenty-four hour, or you die." Lie turned and marched out of the room.

"I think you have put us in hot water," Arjit said softly.

Peter sat at the desk and looked at the controls. "It looks a bit like a TV routing switcher," he said. "It can't be too difficult to figure it out. If only we knew its purpose."

The technology did not look very alien. There were eight rows of twenty-five buttons, each button about an inch square. None of the buttons were illuminated. Carefully Peter pressed one of them. Nothing happened, no sound, no light, no action at all. With carefree abandon, he pressed buttons at random.

No noticeable response, nothing changed at all. It was as if the system had either died or was switched off.

Lie kept his word and kept everyone away from the control room, except Arjit and Peter. Having nothing to do and nowhere to go, all energies were applied to understanding the control panel. For hours, the two systematically tested combinations of buttons. The machine remained totally passive with no noticeable effect. The three pictures stayed unchanged by human influence, and no lights changed on the controls. The lift door closed itself after a given time, with no human prompting.

As the sun sank below the horizon and the ambient light failed, the pictures turned from brilliant colour to black. On one monitor, moonlight could be seen glinting on the still ocean. The others showed darkness. It felt comforting to have some contact with the outside world, even if it had to be through an electronic image. Peter felt happier now that he could tell the difference between day and night without looking at the clock.

The two men slept in the control room. Peter fell asleep at the desk and Arjit curled up on the floor. When they awoke, the screens showed the outside world bathed in daylight. Soon afterwards, one of the guards brought them food and drink from the military kitchen. Again they commenced systematic combinations of the buttons, and again there was no response.

Eventually, Lie and two heavily armed guards arrived. "So?" Lie said. "Demonstrate the use of this equipment."

"I haven't found out how it works yet," Peter complained.

"Oh, great American genius, and you cannot work simple alien device."

"We have not tried all combinations yet. You said twenty-four hours. It's not twenty-four hours, yet."

"You will have your time, then you work the way I say. If you cannot make this thing work, you will dismantle it."

"I thought Chinese were people of infinite patience," Peter said sarcastically.

"I am not Chinese," Lie said proudly. "I am Korean. I have very little patience, as you may soon learn."

Suddenly, the lights in the room dipped to less than half level. The entry door closed and an alarm siren sounded. Peter leapt to his feet. Many of the buttons on the control panel were illuminated and blinking furiously.

"I don't know what I did," Peter said. "But something's happening, and I don't think I like it."

The alarm stopped as the main screen rapidly zoomed into a tiny speck in the sky. The object appeared to be a small twin-engine jet aircraft. The other two screens displayed a slow pan in a circle around the island. Peter pressed some illuminated buttons. Again the machine avoided attempts to communicate. A voice came from the console giving rhythmic orders in a language foreign to all present.

Peter could not understand the display calibrations and therefore had no idea how far away the aircraft could be. The aircraft appeared clearly in the screen; a small passenger plane with its engines mounted at the tail. The plane changed course and began loosing altitude. It was obviously flying an inspection pass of the group of islands to the south.

Lie began barking orders to the guards. A panic ensued. The guards could not leave the room.

"What's happening?" Peter said, raising his voice.

"Mr. Lie wants his men to prepare to shoot that plane down. He thinks it is looking for us. He says it must be from Enright and looking for you."

Suddenly, the lights went out the alarm started again, and the voice began rhythmically chanting. Lights started flashing on the control panel. Peter pressed a few buttons for luck, still nothing obvious occurred.

"I don't know what's happening. But this thing has a good lock on that plane. Look."

Cross-hair graticule with calibrations appeared superimposed over the aircraft. The voice began repeating the same word over and over. The plane got closer and lost even more altitude. Flying only a few hundred feet above the ocean, it tilted to one side giving crew or passengers a good view of the islands beneath its flight path.

The voice stopped. The alarm stopped. All the buttons on the control panel went out. The only sound in the room was the gentle and distant wheeze of the dragon. With a sound like someone striking a low cord on a piano, a bolt of light leapt out at the plane. Smoke and pieces came from the small craft, yet it remained aloft, Modern technology defying the might of the mountain monster.

The dragon's breathing increased its pace. Everyone in the control room became transfixed by the picture on the main screen. Again the low cord struck as a bolt of light hit the aircraft. Pieces were clearly visible falling from the small jet, but it still flew. The dragon was drawing its breath in great gulps, thundering throughout the complex. Other machinery started running in sequence with the monster.

The view screen followed the damaged aircraft, as it appeared to be in difficulties. Its flight path became erratic and lower. The graticule vanished, and the room lights came back on. The dragon obviously felt that it had accomplished its work. The screen continued to track the crippled aircraft as it struck the beach at the south end of the island and disappeared into the trees. Everything in the complex returned to normal. Even the dragon's breath slowed and quietened.

The door opened and the dragon's wheezing diminished. The sound of machinery died away. All the humans in the control room were visibly shaken by the events of the moments before.

"Your demonstration was most effective," Lie said. He marched out of the room and took his guards with him.

"I didn't do it," Peter said. "I didn't do anything, it did it all by itself."

"Was what we saw real, or is it some sort of video game intended to fool us?" Arjit said.

"I don't know. It looked very real to me," Peter said slumping back into the seat. "I guess they'll have to go see if there's an airplane down there on the beach. I can't see anything on the monitor."

Lie took a contingent of twenty men and set out to find the crashed aircraft. He wasn't convinced that what he'd seen on the monitor had been reality. As they rounded the headland, some three hours after the crash, there was no doubt in anyone's mind. Broken pieces of airplane lay scattered on the silver sands. The trees were damaged where a major part of the plane had crashed into them.

It looked as though the aircraft had skimmed the sea, rushed up the beach and bounced off a small uprising of rock. The bounce had smashed the tail off which still lay where it had landed. The bulk of the plane had buried itself in the small forest of palm trees. A woman's body lay face down in the soft sand halfway between the two major pieces of the plane.

Lie walked into the wreckage, looking for clues as to the purpose of the flight. He was convinced that it had to be a spy plane especially when he saw that the registration was Enright Enterprises. Both the pilot and the co-pilot were dead, still sitting in their seats. It was apparent that someone had left the plane. A bloodstained handprint on the bulkhead indicated that it was probably a small person.

Lie quickly gave orders to search for the one or more persons who had escaped the crash. He was afraid the broken plane would be seen from the sky. A detachment of men was dispatched to go back to camp and fetch heavy equipment to remove the wreckage. That evening, after the heavy equipment arrived, a soldier came to Lie carrying the body of a thirteen-year-old boy. He had obviously been injured in the crash and died of his injuries sometime later.

The bodies and all pieces of the small plane were collected and taken to the main camp. The bodies would be disposed of by sea burial. The plane's wreckage was piled up and camouflaged to hide it from the sky or the sea. The sun had set by the time the last piece of aircraft had been hidden. The bodies would be weighted and taken out to sea and dumped after dark.

Peter took the news that it had been a real aircraft to heart.

He felt responsible, as if it had been his fault that it had been shot down. In light of the successful attack Lie recanted his order concerning the control room. Peter and Arjit were left alone to investigate the strange controls in the hope of using the power of the mountain. The machine went back to sleep showing no response to human endeavours. The dragon's breathing slowly died away.

After several days experimenting, Peter discovered the secret of controlling the secondary screens. By using the correct sequence of buttons, he found that he could pan and even zoom in on various targets around the island. Firing the laser, or even controlling the door, remained a secret. The machine seemed to have a will of its own, as if guided by intelligence outside the control room. It reluctantly yielded some control to the humans. Though as if trying to state something, it gave up its secrets only to Peter.

Lie became somewhat friendlier when shown the use of some of the controls. He felt safer and thought that the machine – whatever it was, could be used to protect them from air attack, just as it had destroyed the last aircraft. Work continued on the great doors. Thermal lances and torches were employed to little effect on the unearthly metal. The deeper they penetrated, the greater the difficulty. The inner doors were thicker and of stronger material.

For reasons unknown, the dragon remained hushed. Its wheezing and breathing, almost imperceptible in the depth of the mountain's heart. The sound of machinery died completely away giving the whole complex an eerie and unnerving atmosphere. The control room enforced the quietness with its passive and gradual acceptance of Peter as he slowly discovered the uses of the mysterious control panel.

THE JUDAS FLARE

Chapter 5

L iving in the control room had its disadvantages for Peter and Arjit. Though close to work, it was a long way from any amenity. The nearest washroom facilities were at the bottom near what Peter called the elevator, the one that only he could operate. They set out sleeping bags on the floor for the sleeping period as almost all their waking hours were spent examining the control console and its mysterious workings, trying to find the combinations that would yield full control.

Peter removed some of the covering panels to reveal the inner workings of the machine. Like everything else in the building the interior of the console consisted of glowing cubes – some of them were joined by transparent rods-like devices. The switches on the top of the control panel were miniature cubes, all strung together on a translucent rod. Peter would not allow any of the working parts to be moved for fear of killing the device before he had a chance to understand it. He felt that they could be studied more easily while it was alive and working.

Commander Lie did not believe everyone on the little plane had died in the crash. He sent two, three-man patrols to hunt down and kill any survivors. One party was sent north and the other south. The idea being to sweep back to the centre of the five-mile-long island and thus having the best chance of detecting strangers. The middle, where the dragon mountain stood spanned only one mile wide from coast to coast.

About two days after shooting down the little jet plane, commander Lie visited Peter and Arjit to personally check on the progress they had made with the machine controls.

"Have you mastered this device yet?" Lie said, his eyes twinkling with intrigue.

Peter answered. "No. We can pan the minor screens, though I have no idea how to make it fire or not fire, that's something which, I think, is automatic, and maybe we can't control."

"Look," Arjit said excitedly pointing to one of the minor screens.

Everyone's attention was drawn to the indicated screen. A white flare over the western coast of the island slowly arced and crashed into the sea. Peter quickly manipulated the switches on the control panel. The device zoomed into the picture, revealing two people on the beach. The trees partially obscured the view, though it could clearly be seen that one was a male and the other a female. Both were very young, probably about fourteen or fifteen.

"That is it," Lie yelled, and then he turned and left the room in a terrible hurry.

"He is going to kill them," Arjit said. "Somehow we have to warn them of the great danger they are in."

"I don't know how," Peter said. "How long will it take him to reach them?"

"Less than half an hour. He knows this island and can travel fast over it. You must warn the people on the beach, my young friend, or they too are doomed."

Commander Lie ran to the armoury and took a carbine with hollow point bullets. Wasting no time, he rounded the headlands and skirted along the edge of the mountain. Before reaching the west coast, he met one of his patrols. They did not use radio for fear of giving any passing ship a clue that the island had inhabitants squatting on it.

Lie told two of the men to stand their ground while he went with the third man to hunt the youngsters seen on the beach. In only a few minutes, the two kids were spotted walking toward the central mountain. At almost three hundred yards, Lie stopped, took careful aim, and fired. One of the two children fell, while the other disappeared into the long grass and well out of sight.

"Quickly," Lie said in Korean. "We must catch the other." Lie and the soldier began running toward the downed quarry. Mr. Lie tripped, twisting his ankle. "Keep going. Get that person, I will follow as best I can, but kill them all that you find."

The soldier ran toward where the kids were last seen. With no warning, a girl jumped up from in the long grass only twenty feet ahead of him. Before he could bring his weapon to bear, she raised her hand and fired a signal flare at him. The deadly burning flare struck him in the chest knocking him down. He screamed in terror and pain as the white-hot magnesium melted into his flesh. In only seconds, he suffocated on the deadly fumes from the still burning missile embedded in his body. Commander Lie hobbled forward with his carbine at the ready. The death cries of the soldier angered him and alerted the two men who had been left behind.

The moment he spotted someone squatting in the grass, he fired. The target was not clear with the tall tropical weeds waving in the sea breeze. He fired again and again. Like a gazelle, the girl leapt to her feet and fled toward the trees. At that moment, Lie's men reached him. He fired several more shots, but the girl disappeared into the copse of trees.

"We must get her," he said. "Help me I have injured my ankle."

One of the soldiers helped the commander half-walk, half-hop in the direction the girl had taken. She had run toward the mountain where it sloped down to the western side of the island. As the trio hurried through the wooded area, they spotted two people skulking by some rocks. Fearing that the quarry may be armed Lie stopped. He fired numerous rounds at the position where the two vanished from sight.

After a few moments, he proceeded cautiously. Reaching the base of the mountain slope they found a clear pool of water, which apparently welled up from the ground. The youngsters had completely vanished, there being no apparent hiding place, except the pool. One of the soldiers dropped to his knees and stuck his head into the cold water. He surfaced and wiped his eyes.

"I think they must have hidden in the pool somehow."

"Fool, how can anyone hide in a pool?" Lie snapped.

"There is a cave under the water," the soldier reported.

"You stay and guard this position," Lie took his boots off. "You come with me," he growled at the other soldier.

In only moments, the two were stripped down to their shorts. Still clutching the carbine, Lie slipped into the cold water. He took a breath and dived. The soldier blindly followed. The remaining man stood on guard at the pool's edge awaiting the return of his commander.

None of what had transpired on the western side of the island had been visible from the control room. Peter and Arjit used the scanners with no useful effect. The vegetation impeded the view in many places on the ground.

"If he has harmed those kids," Peter said, "I'll personally kill him with my bare hands."

"Suddenly, the worm turns," Arjit said with a sickly smile. "Now you have the courage to face Lie alone?"

"No. But now there is a reason to face him. He's going to kill us anyway. We have nothing to lose."

"Only our lives."

"We're already dead men. There's no way on earth they will let us go, even if we learn the secret of this place. Especially if we learn the secret of this place because then we'll be a liability and no longer of use to them."

Arjit eased himself down on the corner of the control desk.

"You are right my friend. There is no way out of here. It sounds to me like you have a plan. But should we escape – what of out loved ones?"

"Well yes I have a plan – it's not a good one, it's just the only one I could come up with."

"Do not keep me in suspense."

Peter stroked his chin thoughtfully. "If we can master this apparatus, it will give us power over them. After all, it's probably the most powerful weapon on this planet. It accurately knocked that plane down from miles away, if we could turn it on the rest of them."

"How do we keep them from coming in here and shooting us quite dead?"

"I don't know. There must be a way to close the door. If I could close the door, maybe we'd have a chance."

That night, as Peter lay on his blanket, his thoughts drifted to the idea of escape. There had to be more than one entrance to the complex, probably even entrances that the Chinese guards did not know of. "I'm going to escape," he said softly.

Arjit rolled over to face him. "They leave us alone here because they know there is nowhere for us to go, my friend. How could you escape? They have guns and rockets. They will shoot you with no more thought than they would give to stepping on an ant or swatting a fly."

"True," Peter said. "But I have one advantage over all of them."

"And what, pray, may that be?"

"I can open doors. I just have to touch the glowing panel, and phooey, the door opens. No one else can do that. Not even you."

"How will this help you escape?"

"They're working on that door at the end of the corridor. It's a tough one, but eventually, they'll break through. They will, of course, make me go through it first, just to test the dragon's sting. If you come with me, that's when we'll make our break for it."

"I do not see how that allows you to escape," Arjit said, exhaling loudly.

"Exactly," Peter said excitedly. "Neither do they. If we enter the room, whatever it is, beyond that door, they won't follow us for several minutes being terrified of the dragon sting. That will give us time to look around and see if there is another door with a luminous panel. If there is, we'll waste no time, get the heck to the door open it and run. They'll think we merely vanished, swallowed by the dragon."

"Where will you be running to, my friend?"

"Who cares? They won't be able to follow us. As soon as they try, the sting will kill them."

"They always defeat the sting, and then they will follow."

"True. But we will be safely beyond the next door. It will take them at least another day to cut through that one, and who knows what we'll find on the other side. We may be able to turn this machine against them. We could defeat them all with something from the other side."

"You have been watching too many of you Hollywood movies, my friend. Even if you could get through the next door, and even if you could get this mountain to fight for you, they would still eventually destroy it and you. You would only be delaying the inevitable. Merely a stay of execution, not a reprieve."

"I don't think it's inevitable. There must be the power required to destroy them all, right here in the hollow mountain."

Arjit sighed. "My friend, you must concentrate on your work here. Watch and wait your opportunity. Do not take unnecessary risks. You will get us both killed."

"Why did you kidnap me, Arjit?"

"I did not. I merely asked you to accompany me on a boat trip. Did you not enjoy the ride?"

"No, I didn't, and you did kidnap me, you know you did."

"For that, my friend, I am sorry. You must see I had no alternative. My family, like yours, is being held hostage. This is why I will not help you escape. If you escape, they will blame me, and my loved ones will pay the penalty."

"Well," Peter said, "I'm sorry, but I have to escape before they kill me. They will kill us. You must know that."

"If it is the will of God, then they will. If it is not, then perhaps there is another way out. Perhaps God has in his almighty wisdom a purpose and a plan for us both."

"Oh, yeah! Like what?"

"That I do not, presently, know. God will reveal all, in good time. I do not believe that God would allow you to escape from Vietnam, only to be killed here like a slaving dog."

"I'm not so sure."

"How old were you when you escaped from Saigon?"

Peter thought for a moment or two. "Why?"

"I merely wondered."

"I was ten."

"Then the American soldier could not be your father?"

With a sigh, Peter agreed. "True, though he was an excellent man, he loved me and my mother. He accepted me as his son, which was good enough for me."

"Then his name was not Chan?"

"No. His name was not Chan."

Peter walked to the end of the corridor, where the men were working on the latest door. He wanted to terminate the conversation. He wistfully watched the men at work. Almost any material on earth yields to a thermal lance, yet the unknown metal of these doors totally resists. The lances burned and self-destructed, leaving very little damage to the door material. It was quite spectacular to watch the brilliant light of the lance dull and turn yellow on contact with the door.

After only a short time watching the proceedings, Peter was forcibly ejected from the area. The guards were most uncomfortable having him watch. Perhaps they were on edge because of the tedium and slowness of the progress – commander Lie would be angry.

Sleep was difficult that night, as work on the door at the end of the corridor had intensified. "It would be easier to sleep," Arjit said. "If you could put out this light."

"Yes," Peter said. "But I can't, I don't know how."

"I have been thinking of your idea to pass through the next door," Arjit said slowly.

"Oh, yes. What?"

"Well, have you noticed anything about the doors?"

Peter sat up. "Noticed anything. No, like what exactly do you mean?"

"The illuminated panel that you can touch and open the door. Did you notice they are only on one side of the door? Even the lift only goes one way. You can open it from here, yet not from the other end."

"I don't see any significance in that," Peter said.

"Well, just think of it. You can only go one way. This room, you opened the door. It remained that way, allowing you to exit. Yet when the mountain is under attack, the door closed and there is no way of opening or closing it from in here."

"I'm sorry," Peter said. "I can't see where you are leading me, what's the significance?"

"That's just it. The mountain is trying to lead someone, perhaps you, in one direction. All the doors lead to the interior. If you were already in there, how would you escape, when there is no method of closing or opening a door from the other side?"

Peter thought about it for a moment. Arjit was right. The mountain could resist for prolonged periods, yet it would let him pass without difficulty. "I see there is a conundrum, although I can't see any meaning or sense in it."

"Notice too, the mountain attacks aircraft, but it allows ships to pass unharmed," Arjit said.

"Have you thought of a solution to this mystery, or are you just teasing me?"

Arjit smiled. "I think so."

"Then don't keep it a secret."

"I think the builders of this place were aliens, from another world. They are not here anymore; this place was probably only an observatory. This whole thing is a test, perhaps. It could kill us all by gassing us. It could turn its great weapon against ships that approach. Yet, it supplies us with fresh clean cool air. It supplies us with light to see. Yet will not allow us to learn anything. I think it wants us to do something, something important to it, maybe that is the test. What would a secret mountain want you to do? Think about that."

"I've no idea."

"Perhaps all it wants is to draw us in, there is nothing of value here. It wishes us to think there is. When enough people have done sufficient damage, the mountain will kill us all."

"No, I don't think so. Though it could be alien and maybe it is a test."

"A test, for what?"

"I'm not sure," Peter said. "Perhaps it's looking for intelligence. Possibly the one who solves the puzzle without brute force gets the prize."

Arjit's eyes light up, as a thought struck him. "The cubes tantalize us with promises of great technology, yet they die before our very eyes. Crudity and destruction are impeded, though gentility and intelligence is encouraged. I think it wants you to pass through the doors as you suggested. It wants you to reach the heart. There is something there for you, something that is not for the crude and rough ones of us. Who knows, perhaps in the end, it will kill us all. Or maybe it is salvation."

CHAMBER OF THE GUARDIANS

Chapter 6

Peter felt the small captive world that imprisoned him had begun to close in around him. Unable to speak with anyone except Arjit limited his sociability and increased his isolation. The soldiers were more like automatons than humans. If they were ordered to die, they would obey unquestionably. The infuriating control centre would yield nothing more than partial control of a couple of screens. The tantalizing cubes hid behind non-powered anonymity.

His self-pitying trance became shattered suddenly by the screech of sirens. The next door had been penetrated; a new round of terror, death, and deafening noises would soon begin. Peter trembled, for he knew this was it – his first and maybe only chance to escape. The despicable Chinese inquisitor quickly arrived with his protecting entourage of mute armed slaves, but Mr. Lie remained conspicuous by his absence.

Arjit argued with the newcomers. The confrontation became very heated, and then suddenly one of the guards slammed the butt of his automatic weapon into Arjit's chest. The struggle was brief as two others joined in. The helpless Indian fell to the floor, unconscious. Peter attempted to intervene, and he too was struck by the butts of their weapons. It wasn't possible to argue when the language was totally alien.

They dragged Peter roughly from the control room and marched toward the newly penetrated door. He had no doubt what they wanted him to do. He would once again be the guinea pig. Not only that, but he would have to enter the new area alone. As he approached the gaping hole in the metal door, the guards pulled back. For the first time, Peter saw the fear in their eyes. No one wanted to enter the impending hell zone and die for their troubles.

With a smile of defiance and a flourish of hope, he stepped bravely through the hole. Closing his eyes as he entered the new room, he cringed with the expectancy of the awaiting dragon's sting. All seemed quiet and tranquil as he stood openly in the new area. He opened his eyes and began to take in the scene.

The room looked immense, like an airplane hangar. The lighting came from the same hidden type of luminous tile in the ceiling. On the left wall was a huge, closed door, big enough for a medium-sized aircraft to pass through. It had an illuminated opener panel at the far end. The most amazing things in the almost empty hangar were two huge golden statues.

At either side of a small door stood a giant golden statute of a humanoid. Each idol, a full fifteen feet tall, with two curly cables attached to their navels. The golden images were awe-inspiring and terrible in an undefined way. There were no facial or bodily features just smooth, shining gold. The head had no neck or eyes, or ears or mouth. Looking at them gave Peter chills that ran up and down his spine.

On the ceiling of the hangar were two turrets that followed Peter's movements. The turrets were obviously Dragon stings. Any wrong move could unleash the violent hostility. Peter walked slowly and cautiously toward the gold idols, for a better look at them. The small door between them did not have a lighted opening panel, yet at the far corner of the room was a door that did.

The idols were an enigma for this super hi-tech edifice.

Quite why anyone would build statutes of gold fifteen feet tall, then add red and blue umbilical cords, defied Peter's imagination. He touched one of the idols to see if the feel of the material would yield any further information. It felt hard and cold, just like gold.

The constantly watching death turrets were persistently unnerving. Slowly and almost on tiptoe, Peter walked to the other end of the large room to the lighted panel on the wall. His breath coming in short gulps. Timidly, he put out his hand and pressed it against the panel. With a clang that almost stopped his heart, the great door began to swing away. It opened like a garage door, parking itself against the ceiling of the next room.

The opening had revealed yet another giant chamber, just as wide but only half the length of the first. With his heart pounding louder than anything else in the building, he walked into the new room. As soon as he was well clear of the door, it began closing. With a clang, it closed and the lights dipped. The whole room dropped slightly, then descended. Peter had found the biggest elevator he had ever seen, something akin to the ones used on aircraft carriers.

With a slight clank and a rattle, the room stopped descending, and a door opened on the other side. Bewildered and shocked, Peter walked out and found himself in the very first large room with the burned ceiling. It was the very same room where he had arrived that first fateful night. Some Chinese that were working there were terrified by the new and unusual activity.

Peter felt very uncomfortable as many of the onlookers raised their weapons and pointed them at him. He could not return, having no idea how to operate the elevator. Slowly he raised his hands as a gesture of surrender. No one would enter the elevator to extract him. He was beckoned to leave. Heart pounding and sweat pouring down his face, he walked into the great hall.

Some ruthless guards quickly apprehended him. The great door closed, returning the gallery to its former condition. With much shouting and babbling in Chinese, they pushed him toward the staircase. He walked up and returned to the control room. Peter could understand nothing of what the Chinese soldiers said.

His appearance at the control room door was treated with hostility. People pointed and whispered with eyes wide as though he had performed some miraculous magical trick. There appeared to be confusion, no one understood how he had left in one direction and returned from another.

"Man, are you in trouble." Arjit gasped still in agony.

With an expression of shock or disgust Peter examined Arjit's bleeding eye and ear. "Are you alright?"

"I had hoped you had succeeded, and perhaps they would have killed me and ended this torture."

Arjit's condition angered Peter. "You bastards, leave him alone," he shouted and swiftly received a bang on the chest from an unfriendly rifle butt.

Slumping against the door frame Arjit said, "They thought you had run away. They wanted to take it out on me, as if it were my fault."

"I'm so sorry, Arjit. Your theory was wrong, as the panels lead in a circle. I came back to where I started."

"You must go back into the room, or they will kill both of us."

"I never thought I'd hear myself say this, but I hate these Chinese guys."

Arjit tried to smile. "They are not Chinese, they are Korean. Now go while I can still stand."

"Okay," Peter said softly and began walking toward the burned door. Everyone there stepped back. A body lay in the doorway still smoking from the lightning hit. Missiles had obviously been fired into the hanger, evidenced by the smell of cordite and the black marks on the almost indestructible walls. The air-conditioning efficiently and quickly sucked up and disposed of the smoke.

With his heart pounding like a steam hammer he walked

into the large hangar. Peter reasoned that the room had at one time been used for some kind of flying machine. The massive chamber was perfectly clean – no dust, no oil, not a trace that anyone or anything had ever been there. There were the new marks of missile explosions on the walls. Two rockets had struck harmlessly close to one of the golden idols.

Peter did not fully understand what his captors expected. They obviously felt that he had the ability to distract the stings giving them time to shoot them out of the ceiling. This great room had two and this time they did not track him. They remained pointing at the broken doorway.

Suddenly, a soldier rushed into the room. Before he could fire his missile, he was struck by two bolts of lightning – one from each sting. The noise was horrendous, but the assault did not stop. Two soldiers aimed their weapons inward, one from each side of the broken door. Both stings and both rocketeers fired at once. One rocket found its mark, damaging the sting. Both rocketeers were killed instantly.

The remaining sting went berserk. The small turret fired at an enormous rate. The room became quickly filled with the smell of ozone. The door glowed with the heat of the impacts. Suddenly, the small door between the two idols opened. The room quickly filled with smoke and sparks. There were explosions occurring all around as rockets flew in aimlessly, the men launching them into the chamber and then dying almost instantly.

A ten-year-old child rushed out of the newly opened door and ran toward one of the idols. Peter grabbed him. The two fell to the floor, hot metal sparks falling all around. Confusion and noise filled the room as Peter struggled with the boy, trying to hold, and protect him from the fury of the weaponry and shrapnel. He reasoned that if he could reach the great elevator, they would be safe.

ENDORA

Chapter 7

The sleek Cadillac limousine slid silently to a halt at the main entrance of the Academy for Young Ladies. The summer holidays had arrived and few of the girls remained. Endora and several of her hangers-on descended the stone steps and approached the big-expensive car. Terence, the chauffeur climbed out, opened the boot, and packed the girl's things into it. Endora Elizabeth climbed in the car unaided. Her only concern was putting on a good show for the onlookers, it being important to hold up the queenly image.

Enright had arranged for his only child, Endora Elizabeth Enright to spend the summer holiday in Singapore and Malaya. Lizzie, as she preferred to be called, had reached the great age of fifteen. Overweight and precocious, with short dark hair, her deep brown eyes added a somewhat boyish look. Since her mother had died in a car accident in the Highlands of Malaya, she had moved from one school to another, never settling in, always the rich outsider and able to buy favours.

The Sidney Academy for young ladies is a live-in school that costs more than it's worth. Only the elite rich attend such a place where every whim may be attended. Miss Helen McLean had been engaged as Endora Elizabeth's full-time surrogate parent. Her task, to see that Lizzie had everything she needed. On parent's day, Helen would substitute for absent relatives taking arms full of mostly unwanted presents paid for by the great benefactor in Singapore.

With teary-eyed hand waving and solemn goodbyes the girls became isolated as the electric windows closed, and the car pulled away.

"Where to?" Endora said, fully recovered from the grief of parting.

"Singapore," Helen said.

"Oh, how distasteful. Do we really have to go there, it smells you know?"

"It's your father's wishes."

Endora grimaced. "When isn't it father's wishes? I would rather not spend another boring summer meeting all his old fogies. Can't we go somewhere exciting, somewhere far away from father? Let's go to France, Paris."

"Singapore is exciting," Helen said. "Besides, I'll be with you all the time."

"I thought so. He'll be too busy. He never has time for me. Since Mom died, he's only interested in his work."

"Your father is an important and busy man. You'll understand when you grow up."

"Grow up?" Endora said indignantly. "I'm fifteen years old, I'll have you know. In some countries, that's too old to get married." She pouted and inflated her chest to prove her point.

"You're still a child at heart. Now, please, do be a good girl. We're going to Singapore. Your father ordered it and so it shall be. Now we do have a surprise for you."

"Great, what is it?"

"We'll be going by private plane."

"Father's, no doubt," Endora said with resentment.

"Yes. But that's not the surprise."

"Well, don't sit on it like a cackling hen, what is it?"

"We'll be stopping off in Darwin and picking up some fascinating passengers."

"Oh, God!" Endora said. "Some surprise. A boring bunch

of bloody executives, I suppose. More of father's cronies. Do we have to?"

"You'll see when we get there. I'm sure you'll be surprised."

The limousine eased quietly to a halt at the front door of the Royal hotel, where Helen McLean operated home base in the penthouse. Endora Elizabeth was completely spoiled and all too familiar to the staff at the Royal. Her wardrobe had already been picked out and purchased. What she would take and what she would wear was ready. The suitcases had gone on ahead. The stop at the hotel was merely for freshening and a clothes change.

During the drive to the airport, Endora remained pensive and quiet. She couldn't remember a time when she had been allowed to make a decision for herself, always someone else made all the important decisions. For that matter, she couldn't remember a time when she was allowed to be alone. If it wasn't the busybody teachers, or the monitors, it had to be Helen McLean, guardian and general nuisance.

The flight, though private, had first class priority making passage through the airport officialdom quick and easy. The small exclusive twin-engine jet plane required only a two-man crew. David Boecker, captain and pilot, stood by his machine awaiting his passengers. Endora became enthused when she saw the young handsome twenty-six-year-old pilot standing in his smart uniform.

He looked very elegant in his neatly pressed 'Enright' uniform. "Welcome, Madame," he said to Endora, gently shaking her hand. "I hope you will enjoy the flight."

Her eyes sparkled, and a smile spread across her face. "Thank you, sir" she said and breathed deeply.

With renewed enthusiasm Endora and Helen boarded the small plane. The interior was more like a living room of a luxury cottage than an airplane, with sofa-like seats. Captain Boecker closed and sealed the door, then took up his position beside the co-pilot, Perry O'Neal. In moments, the machine became airborne and speeding on its way to Darwin, approximately a four-hour trip across the parched interior of the Australian continent.

A small galley in a short corridor between the cockpit and the main lounge acted as their airborne kitchen. Endora had developed a crush on the young handsome pilot. She made herself busy preparing a drink in the galley with the full intention of using it as an excuse to talk to Captain Boecker. Being a gentleman and in the employ of Mr. Enright, he gave the girl a quick tour of the plane's controls.

"What's the tiny suitcase?" She said pointing.

"That's an emergency kit. It has a flare gun and cartridges."

"What are they for?" She said brushing her hair with one hand, trying to look alluring.

"Well, in an emergency, you can fire a flare to call for help."

Endora wasn't really interested in flares, or even aircraft controls but the young, handsome pilot consumed her passions. Her fertile imagination already had the young man in compromising situations that Daddy would not approve of.

The flight to Darwin took a little more than four hours. For the latter part of the journey, Endora slept. She didn't like flying, and she didn't want to go to Singapore. As with everyone else in the Enright Empire, there were no other choices. The night passed uneventfully in the Airport hotel. In the morning the aircraft had been serviced and stood on the tarmac ready to fly the last leg of the mission.

Endora and Helen were the first passengers to board and sat comfortably waiting while the engines of the plane supplied power for air-conditioning in the searing heat.

"I want you to be on your best behaviour for this flight, young lady," Helen said.

"Because of the surprise?" Endora quizzed.

"Right. There are three young boys going to join us for the trip to Singapore."

"Oh, no! Three dumbo jocks."

"No. That's why I want you on your best behaviour. The youngest is Horace Granger – ten years old. You must be especially nice to him."

"Why, is he God's chosen or something?"

"Endora, hold your tongue, please. Horace's parents were killed just last week up in Butterworth. It was a traffic accident. Horace knows. He is going to Malaya for the funeral. So be nice to him, be nice for once."

"I will." She sighed deeply.

"Robert Southorn will be spending the summer holidays with you. He is also an orphan. His father worked for your father, and he died two months ago."

"What of?"

"It was an accident in the optics plant. The third one is Sandy Bynum."

"Is he a poor little orphan too?" Endora said sarcastically.

"No. His parents will be waiting for him in Singapore. Now please be nice."

At that moment, the co-pilot arrived with a Darwin employee of the Enright Empire. The man carried a heavy wooden crate, which he placed on the cabin floor.

"We don't want that there," Endora said jumping to her feet and feeling insulted.

"Orders from Mr. Enright," the co-pilot said apologetically.

The employee left and the three boys entered. The first was Robert Southorn a tall blond, blue-eyed lad of fourteen years old. "This is Robert," the co-pilot said.

"Hi," Endora smirked. "I'm Endora Elizabeth Enright. My father owns this plane. You may call me Lizzie."

"Sure. You can call me Digger," Robert said.

"Are you a miner?" Endora asked, deliberately being rude.

"No, it's just a nickname."

"This is Sandy," the co-pilot said introducing the dark-haired youth.

"Hi," Sandy said and wandered off to find a seat.

"This is Horace Granger."

Horace seemed more interested in playing his hand-held video game than talking to any girl, rich or otherwise. Ten-year-old Horace had ample blond hair like Robert, though he was small for his age.

"I'm sorry about your parents," Endora commented lightly.

"Not your business, fatso."

Endora grabbed him by his collar. "Listen barf breath, this is my plane. You are less than a worm. Be polite, or I'll throw you off, and if you're luck that'll be before we take off."

"Drop dead, sheila," he said, then walked off and threw himself onto one of the plush seats. "Let's move this crate before the sheila blows her cork or somethin'."

"Ignore Friz," Digger said.

"Friz, Friz!" Endora Elizabeth echoed. "Why Friz? Is he frizzy round the edges, or something?"

Digger smiled. "No, he was a Frisbee champion, that's why they call him Friz."

Endora sat down. She felt sorry for the kid, yet she still hated the insufferable little jerk. Horace Granger began a long and deliberate ignore. He turned up the volume on his hand-held game and played to the annoyance of everyone else.

"This flight is going to take more than five hours," Endora said raising her voice. "Do I have to put up with that child making all that disgusting noise?"

"Please have patience, Endora," Helen said. "You know he's recently lost his parents. Be nice to him."

The small plane took to the sky, and Endora reached the point where she could no longer stand the incessant electronic music and strange sound effects. She stood up and walked over to Horace. "Listen Frizzy, or whatever the hell your stupid name is, cut out the crap, or I'll make you eat that thing."

"Shut up and leave me alone, sheila."

"I'm not bloody Sheila. Now listen you little snot rag, this is my father's plane. Even that game was made by his company. If you don't cut it out, I'll do something you'll be sorry for."

"Drop dead, fat arse."

Endora snatched the game from the boy's hands. She switched it off and handed it back. "I'm slowly losing my temper with you. I am trying to be nice. But don't push me too far, or I'll have you thrown off the plane."

"Bloody sheila," he said and turned his game on again.

Digger slipped in between them and turned the volume down. "Come on, Friz. We've got a long way to go. Don't aggravate the fat sheila."

In one shot, Endora gave Digger a left cross, knocking him clean out of the seat. Helen leapt to her feet in an attempt to referee the fight, but it was all over. Endora walked to the galley, trying to calm down. She hated all the kids. As she reached the galley, she turned. "I hope you all die of a deadly and painful disease."

HOPE ISLAND

Chapter 8

After the initial outburst of hostilities, everyone aboard the little plane settled down to quiet boredom. Horace kept his volume down to a polite level. Sandy Bynum remained very quiet and kept much to himself. Endora and Digger, being of similar age, got along quite well. All seemed tranquil until the pilot made an announcement.

"Ladies and gentlemen, we are now passing the southern tip of the Banda Sea. If you look out the starboard side, you will see several groups of islands in the distance. These were all occupied by the Japanese during World War Two."

Endora walked to the cockpit in order to converse with the pilot. "Were all the islands occupied? I mean, like all of them?" she asked.

"Oh yes. Just over there is a group of islands," he said, pointing. "Where you can still see the sunken ships. A mate of mine and me found them one summer. We were spending our holidays on his father's yacht. It's not too far off our regular course."

"And you can see under the water?" Endora's eyebrows rose in surprise, the thought of seeing sunken ships intrigued her.

The pilot smiled. "Sure, I'll show you. It's only a little off our course. See that bunch of islands over there?" He pointed.

Endora leaned over his shoulder in order to gain a better look through the front window and to get closer to the handsome pilot. "Oh yes, I see them. Is that where the ships are?"

"I'll take it, Perry," the captain said to his co-pilot. With that, David gently eased the stick to the right and down. The small plane began loosing altitude and swooped toward a small archipelago in the vivid blue sea.

Endora's interest peaked as ships became visible, nestling under the crystal-clear water. "How did they get there?" She asked.

"Most of them were bombed by our boys after the battle of the Coral Sea."

There was a blinding flash and the small plane shuddered violently. The sound of the engines changed abruptly, and an alarm sang out. Endora Elizabeth almost fell onto the control panel as the plane shook. "What's happening?" she gasped. "Have we hit something?"

"Go to your seat and strap yourself in," David said calmly as if the incident were a routine happening.

Endora pulled back and as she did so, she saw what looked like a lightning bolt rush up from the island ahead and strike the aircraft. All the lights went out, and the airplane became very unstable.

"The elevator's damaged. I can't hold it. Our only hope is the island ahead," the pilot said. His voice was still firm and reassuring.

Endora Elizabeth hurriedly threw herself into the first seat near the galley and strapped herself in. "Strap yourselves in," she yelled excitedly. "We're going to crash. We're going to crash."

All electrics were out – no lights, nothing. The pilot yelled back to his passengers. "Don't worry, we'll be alright. Our best hope is the island ahead. Please brace yourselves for the impact. I'm heading for the beach."

The aircraft became unstable as it bobbed and pitched on its erratic course. Endora could see the ocean dangerously close through the side window. Helen became terrified and began to cry. Endora felt paralyzed with the fear of what was about to happen. Digger had curled up with his hands round the back of his head.

"This is it, hang on everybody," the pilot yelled.

Elizabeth felt that her head would explode with the confusion and fear that filled it. Suddenly, the plane jerked violently with a terrible roar of grinding metal and breaking glass. It sounded like thunder from the inside of a storm. The violent movement increased, as did the sound. All at once, darkness and silence embraced the survivors. The terrible grinding of metal and shattering of glass had stopped, and the world seemed totally and unnaturally silent.

Endora Elizabeth felt sick and dizzy. Slowly she opened her eyes. The sight that met her gaze was more horrifying than the crash itself. The plane had broken into two. Only a great hole remained where Helen had been sitting. The girl sat looking trying to comprehend what had happened. A trail of debris lay scattered across the sandy beach, luggage, and pieces of aircraft everywhere. The silence became near overwhelming. Endora glanced around thinking there were no other survivors.

Slowly, the young-frightened girl climbed to her feet, trembling with shock and fear. Sandy Bynum stood and faced her. His face covered in blood. Without a word, the boy fled from the broken aircraft and ran into the jungle. Endora felt the pain in her left shoulder and touched the blood trickling from her right ear. Slowly she looked around. Friz had disappeared and so had Helen. Digger sat slumped in his seat.

Gingerly, she walked into the cockpit. Both men were deathly still. Trembling with fearful anticipation, Endora touched the pilot's neck. No sign of a pulse. He had slumped over the controls in the crash. With the windshield smashed and the co-pilot's body draped across the dash, the scene terrified Endora. With her ear to the pilot's back she listened for signs of life – there were none. Endora decided that the flight crew were beyond anyone's help.

Trembling and with eyes wide, she backed out of the

cockpit. A groan from behind made her turn sharply, Digger moved. Quickly, she rushed to his side. "Digger, are you all right?" she said with her voice almost at panic pitch.

He groaned and opened his eyes. "Am I still alive?"

"Yes, I can't find Friz or Helen and Sandy ran into the jungle. What are we going to do?"

"What about the crew?"

"They're dead."

With a wince and a groan, he unbuckled the belt and stood up. "We should assess the situation," he said, in his most manly voice.

Together, they walked from the wreckage. The tail section lay some distance away on the beach. A female body reclined on the sand as if asleep in the warm tropical sun. "It's Helen!" Lizzie yelled, running to the prostrate woman. She appeared to be dead. Lizzie began weeping and kicked the corpse. "You stupid old cow, where are you when I need you?" She kicked the body again and again losing control of her emotions.

"Stop it, you fat idiot," Digger yelled and slapped her face.

Lizzie fell to her knees and sobbed uncontrollably. Digger's heart raced. Somehow, he had to take charge of the situation and do something sensible, something heroic and manly, something to save them all. "Come on. We've got to save ourselves," he said, trying to sound officious and adult.

"How could it happen?" she sobbed. "How could such a thing happen?"

"Come on, we've got to get organized."

"How could it happen? A few minutes ago we were safe and happy, now the whole world has fallen apart." The tears poured down her face.

"Don't be so bloody melodramatic, Lizzie. Come on, we've still got to find Friz and Sandy."

Endora slowly stood up. "I hate everybody. My mother left me when I needed her most. Now Helen's left me and you called me fat. Just who do you think you are?"

"She didn't leave, she's dead. Now pull yourself together.

Your father will soon be looking for us. We'd better be ready. When the rescue planes arrive, we'll need to signal them."

"No he won't. He might send some representative, but he won't come himself. He doesn't have the time for me."

Digger took her hand in an attempt to comfort her. "Come on. We'll set up camp in the plane."

"No," she said emphatically. "There are dead people in there."

"So? We'll move them."

"No, we'll camp out here."

"There are dead people out here too," Digger said.

"I don't care. I don't want to go back in there. I can't."

"Alright, Lizzie, we must get some things. There's food in the galley. Come on. You've got to help me. We must work as a team."

Together, they walked to a major part of the wreckage. Lizzie slowly conquered the shock and fear of her new situation. When they reached the plane, Friz was rooting about in some of the dross and luggage. He looked up and saw the couple. "Your bloody father's going to pay for this," he said.

"What are you talking about, you silly child?" Lizzie snapped.

"Look," he said, holding out his hand-held video game. "It's busted. You'll pay for this." There were tears in his eyes.

"You stupid dickhead," Endora said. "The plane crashed. We were shot down, or hadn't you noticed all the wreckage?"

"It was lightning," Friz said. "I saw it. It was lightning. And you'll still pay."

"We were shot down, now shut your face, or I'll shut it for you, you half-baked little wimp."

"Couldn't have been lightning," Digger said. "It was and still is a clear sky. You don't get lightning on a clear day."

"We were shot down," Lizzie demanded. "I saw the missile streak across the sky and hit us. I was in the cockpit; I saw it all happen."

Digger's eyebrows wrinkled with thought. "We were hit

twice,"

Lizzie noticed the wooden crate that had been loaded aboard in Darwin. "Look," she said pointing to it. "It's broken open."

Digger examined the spilled contents of the crate. It was an extremely fine white powder. "Holy mackinaw! It's dope. Heroin. Your old man's a drug runner."

"He wouldn't do that," Lizzie said. "He just wouldn't"

"Well, what's this?"

Lizzie examined the white powder. She put a tiny amount to her lip. "God, it tastes terrible," she said, spitting the substance out.

"Drugs," Digger said. "You were right, Lizzie. Someone fired two missiles at us, and they intended to shoot us down. It's probably a drug war. Your father didn't know anything, but the pilot did. That means that we could be in more trouble. Whoever shot us down will be after that dope. We'd better get out of here before they find us."

"Alright, let's take what we need and get out of here," Lizzie concurred.

For once, they were all in agreement. The possibility of the people who shot down the plane coming for them frightened the children. Quickly, they began gathering things that might be useful. Endora went into the cockpit. The small suitcase containing the flares and flare gun was still strapped to the wall. She removed it, took one last look at the dead crew, and fled from the plane.

"We'll need food," Digger said. "Get the food from the galley."

"You get it."

Minutes later, the three survivors were walking away from the plane wreck and toward the jungle. In the distance they could see the peak of a small mountain.

"We'll head for that hill," Digger said. "We should be able to find some shelter there."

"We should stay by the plane," Lizzie said. "They won't

know where to look for us."

"That's the whole point," Digger snapped. "We don't want anyone to find us. We'll find them. When the search plane comes, we'll signal it, if it's one of ours. If it's the drug lords, we stay hidden. We don't want them to find us."

"How will we know if it's ours?" Friz said.

Digger exhaled loudly. "What do you think, dickhead?"

"I don't know."

"It'll be Royal Australian Air Force; they don't run drugs. Or it could be Elizabeth's father's plane."

"You owe me a video game," Friz said, elbowing Endora.

"You're a pain in the neck!" she snapped. "How come you didn't get killed in the crash like a good boy?"

Soon they reached a low cliff that stretched up above them. "This is great," Digger said, admiring the natural formation. "We'll only have to guard one approach. The next thing is to find water. We could be here for several days."

Lizzie slumped to the ground. "Let's have one of those sandwiches. We haven't had lunch yet."

"I don't know how you could eat under these circumstances," Digger said. "I'm too scared to eat anything."

"I'll eat yours," Friz said, putting out his hand for a sandwich.

"This camp site will do for today." Digger, sat on the ground. "Tomorrow we'll have to find a proper one."

"What d'yah mean, a proper one?" Endora said, with a mouthful of sandwich.

"We must find a place close to the sea, close to fresh water and close to an open space."

"Oh, yeah, and why's that?"

"If there's a ship, we'll need to be able to light a fire or signal it somehow. If it's a plane or a helicopter, we'll need to be able to wave to it. And, of course, we won't last very long if there's no fresh water."

"I'd like a drink, now," Friz said.

"Drop dead, dummy," Endora growled. "We don't have

anything to drink."

It all seemed like a dream. Everything had become peaceful and quiet. The weather was pleasant, the sunlight warm, the trees were green and friendly. Under other circumstances, it would have been a veritable paradise.

"We'll be alright," Digger said. "I'm a Boy Scout and I know how to survive here. They'll miss us when the plane doesn't arrive, then they'll start the search for us. You'll see it won't be long, maybe just a couple of days."

"Look what I've got," Lizzie said, opening the small suitcase.

Digger smiled as he recognized the items. "A flare pistol, and two flares. Smart thinking, that's just what we need."

DEADMAN'S CAVE

Chapter 9

The sun began setting in the western sky, casting long, rosy shadows across the little island. Endora said, "I've never slept outdoors before. We have to keep the wild animals away, we'll have to light a fire,"

"Oh no, we won't," Digger snapped adamantly. "No fires. The smoke will give our position away to the drug lords."

Endora whined. "What about wild animals?"

"There are no wild animals on these islands. Did you see any?"

"Even my father would never expect me to sleep on the cold ground, what shall I use as a bed?" Her eyes were wide with an expression of horror.

Friz laughed. "Maybe with his money, he'll have the island upholstered for you. We'll call it Lizzieville."

"You stupid little dingo. Why don't you run off and get yourself eaten by some horrible wild animal or something."

"Alright, you two," Digger said. "Let's not fight. We've got problems enough here. Now, the ground isn't cold. This happens to be a tropical island. If the weather holds, there'll be no difficulties. The sand's nice and warm and soft."

"No problems," Endora said raising her voice, "how can you say no problems? We've crashed on some unknown, uncharted island in the middle of nowhere. There are dangerous drug smugglers after us and no one knows where we are. For all you know that hill is a Volcano and getting ready to explode. We'll all probably get murdered in our sleep, and you say we have no problems."

"Alright, so we have a few problems."

"I've got to have a pee," Friz said.

"So what you want, stupid? You want I should hold your little hand for you?" Lizzie barked at the small kid.

Friz ran off into the dense wood just to their left. "Don't try to hide from me, you lot," he yelled back. "It's not funny."

Endora sat on the ground. "I think we'll all die here. They'll never find us. We'll end up like the Swiss Family Robinson."

"Don't be silly. By tonight, they'll know for sure we're missing. They'll start a search first thing in the morning. Within two hours, the sky here will be buzzing with planes looking for us."

"It's all my father's fault," she said. "His laziness, his stupidity. He couldn't come to see me, oh no I have to cross half the world, so he looks like a good father. I hate him. I really, really hate him."

"No, you don't, not really."

"Yes, I do. He's a selfish pig. Mom died because of him, now I'll die, probably eaten by ants or snakes or something." She ripped the necklace from her neck. "He gave me this stupid thing. Well, actually, he got someone else to give it to me. He was too busy to do it himself. I don't want it." She flung the necklace pendant away just as Friz arrived.

The young lad walked to where the jewellery fell to the ground and picked it up. "Don't you want it?"

"No, I don't."

"Can I have it, then?"

"Keep the bloody thing. It's junk anyway."

Friz examined the pendant, smiling. "Cool! I found that Bynum kid."

"Where?" Digger said in surprise and jumping to his feet.

Friz pointed. "He's over there."

Elizabeth got up and together with Digger they walked in the direction indicated by Friz. Just beyond the clearing in the woods, they spotted Sandy sitting at the base of a tree. He didn't move, just remained perfectly still, propped up against the palm. The two walked over to him. He did not look natural, more like a doll placed there by someone.

"Sandy," Digger said, poking the boy with one finger. There was no response.

Endora knelt to face him. As she looked into the boy's face, the reason for his quietness became obvious. "He's dead," she said softly.

He had caked blood in his ears and on his chin. The lad had died from internal injuries received in the crash. His eyes were still open, blank and staring.

"Come on," Digger whispered. "We should leave him."

Lizzie stood up, she sighed. "Until today, I'd never seen a dead person. We should bury him. We can't leave him like that, something might eat him."

"We don't have a spade or the time. Let's get back to Friz. We should all stick together if we intend to survive until the rescuers get here. Sandy's beyond our help, there's nothing we can do for him."

When they arrived back where they had left Friz, he was nowhere to be seen. "Friz," Endora yelled. "Friz where are you?"

"Quiet," Digger snapped. "If Friz can hear you, so can whoever's looking for us."

"I hope nobody's looking for us."

"Nonetheless, don't shout like that. He couldn't have got far. We'll find him in silence. Keep your eyes and ears open. We'll walk that way." He pointed. "If we don't find him, we'll walk back again, alright?"

Quietly, the two walked along the cliff face through the forest of tropical trees. The plan was simple. As long as they stayed close to the cliff, they couldn't get lost. Returning would merely be a case of walking the other way. After approximately half-an-hour, Friz came walking toward them from the direction of the woods.

"Where the hell have you been?" Digger said. "To survive, we have to stick together. I don't want you wandering about this place."

"Sorry," Friz said. "I won't get lost. I found us a cave."

After a small discussion on the dos and don'ts of jungle survival, they set out to explore Friz's cave. They walked for about five minutes, then Friz stopped and pointed. Digger and Lizzie looked in the direction he pointed. There was a ledge some thirty or forty feet up the side of the cliff. On the ledge was a cave, though it looked small and uninviting.

"We can't get up there," Digger said. "And we can't camp here. We have to find fresh water. This is not a good spot at all."

"No need, gees keep your hair on." Friz said. "Haven't you ever heard of coconuts?"

"Yes," Digger replied. "But, have you ever tried to open one?"

"Yes. My friend Abdul showed me how. If you get the nut, then I'll open it for you."

The challenge was set. Finding a coconut tree was easy. Extracting a nut from the tree presented a different problem. After repeated attempts to climb up one of the palm trees that lay at a slight angle, Digger decided that it was impractical, and they didn't have the tools to cut it down. Lizzie came running excitedly. She had a windfall in her arms.

Friz took the nut and shook it. "Might be alright," he said, and started work opening it. He held the nut in both hands and repeatedly bashed it against the sharp corner of a rock. After a few minutes, the husk came loose enough to be pulled off. He took a shut knife from his pocket and stabbed the nut in the monkey face. "Here," he said, handing it to Lizzie, "sheilas first."

She took it. "What do I do with it?"

Friz laughed for the first time since the crash. "You don't know what to do with it? What; a sheila don't know! Everyone knows what to do with it."

"Well, I don't," she said indignantly, "I do not know what to do with it. This is the first time I've lived in a jungle."

Friz shook his head. "It's your nut, or I'd drink it myself. You guys don't know anything. There's milk in there. Suck the hole."

"It's dirty, you don't know where it's been."

Friz grabbed the nut. He turned it over and shook it. "See, it's full of milk. It's good stuff, you can drink it. It's perfectly clean an' it's only been in the husk." After draining some of the liquid, Friz broke the shell. The coconut meat made a welcome repast that all the children could enjoy.

Digger and Endora sat on the ground and ate the fresh food as Friz began scaling the cliff face. The climb presented almost no problem for a youngster. The rock face leaned at about thirty degrees with plenty of steps. After a while, he reached the cave, which turned out to be not much more than a hole in the side of the mountain. The boy crawled in, and after some four or five minutes crawled out again.

"Come on mates. It's easy," he yelled down encouragingly.

Digger and Lizzie began the climb to meet Friz. "This will ruin my hands," she complained.

"Like that's really something to worry about," Digger said. "I don't want him shouting to all and sundry, he'll attract attention."

In a short time, they reached Friz, who was patiently waiting by the hole in the mountain. "Have you been in?" Lizzie said peering into the darkness.

"Sure."

"What's in there?"

"Just electric light and some dead men."

"You stupid sod. What's in there?"

"Go find out for yourself."

Lizzie crawled into the hole. She could see nothing in the total darkness. It felt very scary – she backed out again. "I can't see anything. I don't think there's anything in there at all you are a little liar."

"Let me go first," Digger said taking up position in the tunnel. Slowly, he crawled into the murky darkness. After a few seconds, he found the end of the tunnel. A black void extended beyond the crawlway. "There's nothing there but a big hole," he yelled. "I think the mountain's hollow."

"Step down into the room," Friz yelled. "I did."

Lying on his stomach, Digger reached in and found the floor about eighteen inches below the hole. Climbing in carefully, he was able to stand. Endora crawled in after him, the presence of the courageous Digger helped dispel her fears. He helped her down onto the hard floor. Both stood in the gloom unable to see.

"Some electric light," Lizzie said. "It's darker than the black hole of Calcutta in here."

Horace began climbing along the tunnel. His body near to filling the hole cut off most of the light that had been filtering into the chamber. "Where's the light gone?" He said as he reached the end of the tunnel.

"There is none, you dingo," Lizzie snapped. "You are an idiot."

"There was last time I was here." He climbed into the room. As soon as he stood vertical, the light came on.

Lizzie jumped and screamed at the sight of the skeletons on the floor, clad in tattered clothing with old rusty weapons lying by their sides. She suddenly dashed for the hole and made a fast exit.

"Wicked," Friz said. "Real wicked. Have you ever seen anything like it? Wow!"

Digger made a cursory examination of one of the skeletons. "They're Japanese soldiers. Probably died here during the war. Could be disease or any kind of thing. Come on we'd better get out of here, it's most likely not safe."

"Cool," Friz said with a big smile on his face. "Real cool."

The light came from behind the translucent ceiling. "Where's the light switch?" Digger said.

"Don't know. The light just comes on when you get here."

"We better get out of here. This place could be deadly. Who knows what they died of?"

"Can I keep one of the skulls?"

"No, you little ghoul. Come-on, let's get out of here."

As Friz climbed back into the tunnel, the chamber light switched off. Now aided by a fearful urge, Digger pushed the kid to accelerate his departure. "Come on. Let's get the heck out of here. Lizzie needs us, she's only a girl."

Elizabeth stood outside, her eyes wide and staring. The experience in the cave had frightened her. "I hate you Horace Granger," she growled.

Friz laughed at her cowardice. "Wet your knickers, did you? Them dead guys will be creeping up on you while you're asleep at night."

"I'll throttle you, you little dingo," she yelled.

Digger looked up at the mountain. "I think we should go back the way we came and get to the coast. There's no chance of camping here."

"I'm with you," Endora said.

Again the trio set out in an attempt to find a camp for the night. Soon they passed close to the spot where Sandy had been found sitting at the base of a tree. A few moments beyond, Digger decided that they had found a good enough place to camp. The children were tired, frightened, and eager to rest. As the sun sank below the mountain, the group huddled close together at the base of the cliff.

"Listen," Friz said. "There's an engine running somewhere."

They all listened. "I can't hear anything," Digger reported.

"Me neither," Lizzie agreed.

"Put your ear to the rock," Friz said in a whisper. "Listen, you can hear it in the distance, like a ship's engine running."

Digger put his ear to the rock. Sure enough, he could hear the far-away sound of a steam engine quietly purring away. "It must be the generator that made the light in the cave."

"That means that we are not alone," Endora said in a hoarse whisper. "Someone has to look after the engine."

Digger agreed and suggested they take turns at watch. He decided that he would take the first watch. Sleep for everyone came in fits and starts. Fear of the unknown, accompanied by the constant puff, puff of the unseen engine, placed a strain on the children. None were used to sleeping under the stars and hearing the sounds of strange insects, and a big engine wheezing away deep in the bowels of the earth created visions of monsters and nasty things that walk at night.

When the morning dew fell and a slight chill took to the air, all three were sound asleep. Friz opened his eyes before the others. He looked around, stood up and observed his companions, then reassuring himself that they were still alive. He wandered off searching for fallen coconuts or any other edible offering. The other two remained snoring, oblivious to the world around them.

Some time later, Friz came running through the woods yelling for the others. The noise he made woke them. "Quiet," Digger growled. "You'll tell the world where we are."

Lizzie jumped up. "What's wrong, what's happening?"

"It's Sandy, he's gone. He's one of the undead. He's walked off. Gone."

Lizzie smirked: "You twit. How could he? He's dead, isn't he?"

"He's not there. He must have walked off, he's not there. I tell you he's disappeared."

"No," Digger demanded. "He didn't walk off, someone found him. We should get back to the plane. Maybe the rescuers are here. Might be they arrived during the night and didn't see us."

"Could be the drug smugglers are here," Lizzie whispered.

"No, they wouldn't take the time. What would they want with a dead kid? It must be the rescue party. Maybe a boat pulled in during the night, that's why we didn't hear it."

"Or some horrible, people eating monster," Lizzie said with wide eyes.

"No, it's got to be the rescuers."

"Could be the engine we heard," Friz said. "Perhaps they have a machine with them."

Digger exerted his authority in a manly voice: "Right! Grab all your bits. We've got to get to the plane."

Quickly, they collected their meagre possessions and began the trek to where they thought the plane should be. It took them almost an hour to reach the beach location, but still no aircraft could be seen.

"It's gone," Digger said, genuinely amazed and spinning around to cover all the area. "Where could it have gone? Planes don't vanish."

Lizzie blinked and looked about. "We must have the wrong place, it crashed somewhere else."

"No," Digger said, his eyes wide and searching. "Look, there's where the nose dug into the sand. There's the deep trench."

The thought of some terrible force removing all the dead and the broken plane terrified the gang. Visions of giant monsters pervaded their imaginations. There was obviously a lot more to the island than showed on any map.

THE LIMPID LIGHT

Chapter 10

Fear compelled the youngsters to run back into the cover of the forest. The trees at least seemed to offer some protection from whatever stole the plane. They retreated the way they came, back toward the cliff face.

"I can't understand what could have happened to the plane," Digger said. "It would take days to clear up all that wreckage. Where could it have gone? And you'd think there would be bulldozer tracks and stuff."

Endora looked angry and felt insulted that no rescue had occurred. "You said there would be planes looking for us this morning. I don't see any. My father's never where he's needed." Her voice quavered as tears began to flow.

"Don't be so stupid. It's not his fault. They'll come; you'll see."

"I hate you; I hate you all."

Friz laughed. "Money don't do anything here, does it, fatty?"

She attempted to lash out at him, but he ran faster than she could. "I hate that little dingo," she said venomously.

Digger felt just as afraid as any of them, yet he wanted desperately to be the superior, calm, steadfast and fatherly figure the kids would look up to. "I'd like you two to stop fighting.

We've got to work with each other for survival."

At length, they reached the cliff. Digger decided they should go the opposite way from the day before. Horace kept well clear of the others. He was afraid that Endora would hit him if she could get close enough. The cliff sloped gently downwards from the mountain toward the sea. At the end of the cliff they found a crystal-clear pool where the water welled up out of the ground and flowed in a small stream to the sea.

"Wow," Friz said. "What a cool place to drown worms."

"You stupid little dickhead," Endora screeched. "This is drinking water. You'd better not try drowning anything in it."

"He means fishing," Digger said. "This will be a good place to camp. It's not far from the sea. It's close to the trees and there's lots of drinkable fresh water. You guys agree or what?"

Lizzie eyed the water suspiciously. "How do you know it's fit to drink?"

Digger knelt down and tasted it. "Yes," he said, smiling. "It's perfect. Tastes better than bottled water, and it's cool."

The water looked clear and tasted sweet and felt cold. Where it overflowed, it caused a small stream that ran eventually to the sea making it easy to find this place. The rest of the day passed slowly. No rescue planes flew over – in fact, no planes at all were seen in the sky. Food was moderately boring, coconut and banana shoots. Digger found a tapioca tree, but no one knew exactly what to do with it.

The night came as eerily as it had the night before. Sitting near the base of the rock unnerved the children for it amplified the night sounds. Slowly and deliberately, the dragon wheezed in the distance. "Look," Horace yelled suddenly. Standing by the limpid pool his face was illuminated by an eerie light that came from the water.

Digger moved close to Friz. "What is it?"

"Look, there in the water – something shiny."

The pool had an unusual luminescent quality, though from where he was, Digger could not see the cause. "Perhaps it's radioactive."

"That's good," Endora said sarcastically. "You've been drinking it. I suppose it will be handy if you start glowing in the dark, we won't lose you."

Digger was not amused at the thought that he may have already been poisoned. "Horace drank some, too," he said softly.

"It looks like a light to me," Friz said. "When the sun's up, I'll go have a look at it."

The rest of the night passed uneventfully, though the whole group worried about the water. If it should turn out to be radioactive, they could not drink it and would have to find some elsewhere else. As soon as the sunlight struck the ground, Lizzie awoke. Friz was nowhere to be seen, though Digger lay close by snoring like a buzz saw.

Horace turned up with a broken coconut. "I've got your breakfast," he said.

"Oh stuff it, I don't want any more coconut. I'll turn into a monkey," she said, trying to show disgust.

"You already are a monkey."

"I'm going to kill you, you dickhead."

"You have to catch me first, fatty."

She ran after him, but Horace was far too fast for her. "I'll get you when you come back, you little dingo."

The noise woke Digger. "Can't you two get along like adults? You're always squabbling, like babies."

"It's him. I'm going to bash his head in."

"No you're not. Act sensible. Act your age. He's only a kid. He doesn't know any better."

Only a few minutes later, Horace came back. He knew that Digger would protect him. Unexpectedly, he pulled off his shirt and slipped into the pool. "Poh! It's cold."

Lizzie was horrified. "That's drinking water. Get out. I can't drink Horace-alution."

"Shut up, fatty." He took a deep breath and submerged.

Lizzie was annoyed, and by the time she reached the water, Friz had vanished from sight. She gazed into the pool. It looked clear and clean, and with no sign of the irksome child. "He's drowned," she screamed.

Digger ran to the side and looked into the water. Sure enough, Friz had disappeared from the face of the world. "He's got to be there somewhere. I mean, how long can he hold his breath?"

"I don't know. You better go after him."

"I can't swim. I can't go after him."

Lizzie felt the water. It was freezing. "I'm too frightened to follow. Maybe he's dead. Could be the dragon got him."

Digger sighed loudly. "There ain't no dragon."

As the two knelt by the water, Horace suddenly reappeared and noisily burst through the surface of the pond. "Hi," he said, shaking the water from his eyes.

Digger extended a hand and helped Friz out. The kid was shaking, his teeth chattering. "Where were you? You scared us half to death."

Friz began drying himself with his shirt. "There's a cave in there and some other stuff."

"What other stuff?"

"You'll have to come with me to see for yourself."

"I can't," Digger said. "I can't swim."

"You don't have to swim. Just hold your breath. It's only four or five feet deep. There's nothing to it. Even fatso could make it."

Lizzie walked behind him and grabbed him by the hair. "I've got you. Do I kill you here and now? Or do you apologize?"

"For what?"

"If you make inference to my weight just once more, I'll put my hand down your throat and carefully and slowly remove your tonsils with my fingernails."

"Okay. I promise I'll be nice to you if you come with me into the secret lagoon."

"Where?"

"In the secret lagoon. It's really cool."

She thought about it for a few moments. "Well only if you go first. I'll follow you. And if you try anything I'll bash your brains out."

"No," Digger said. "I don't want either of you going in there. Just tell us what you found. Where does the light come from?"

"Well," Friz said. "I can't tell you; you'll have to see for yourself."

Lizzie took a deep breath. "Lead the way. I'll follow you. I'm not afraid of anything you can face."

Friz threw his shirt on the ground. "Come on, then." He slipped into the water, took a deep breath and disappeared under the surface.

"Don't go," Digger said softly.

"I have to. Dickhead's already gone." She slipped off her shoes and climbed into the cold water. "Ho, it's cold." She took a deep breath and disappeared under the surface. Following Friz down into the water, through the arch, and up into a new brightly lit chamber. When she broke surface and wiped her eyes, Friz was standing in the sterile room. Quickly, she pulled herself from the cold water.

At the far end of the room stood a door with a small luminous square button. The water welled up from a hole, then flowed downhill through a channel and vanished into the pool from which she had emerged. The room looked clean and neat and unused. The light came from an evenly lit ceiling. Two skeletons lay on the floor.

"What's that?" she demanded angrily.

"Dead men," Friz said with a smile.

"Well it doesn't frighten me, but I don't like this place. How come the water goes down there, is it magic or something?"

Frizz shrugged. "I guess this room is higher than the water outside."

"This place is man-made. It's not natural."

In the strange chamber the dragon resonated as it breathed. Friz smiled; he enjoyed teasing Endora. "Cool," he said. "Real cool."

"What is?"

"Woo. I mean wow! I can see your nipples."

Lizzie looked down. The water had made her light cotton dress almost completely transparent. She felt suddenly embarrassed. Even though she wore a bra, it too, was almost invisible. Being partially overweight, she had more bosom than the average girl of her age. Clutching her breasts with her hands in an attempt to hide them, she swore at Friz, turned her back and slipped into the water. Seconds later the girl surfaced outside.

"Hand me Friz's shirt," she said clinging to the edge of the pool.

Digger gave it to her. "What d' you want this for?"

"Be a nice boy. Turn you back."

Digger did as he was asked. Quickly, she climbed out of the water, just as Friz was surfacing. She stretched the shirt around the front of her and tied the arms behind her back.

"You missed it all," Friz said excitedly.

"What?" Digger asked.

"She showed me her boobs."

"I'll kill you, you little dingo." Throwing a handful of sand at him as he climbed from the water, she rushed forward and smacked him so hard in the face he fell over backwards.

Digger intervened. "Stop it. He's only a kid, ignore him. He just does it to get your dander up. Now back off."

Horace got up and ran into the forest. Lizzie felt angry and embarrassed. Her dress remained transparent because of the water it retained. Without a word, she walked in the direction of the woods. The girl had little idea how to conduct herself in the presence of the opposite sex. In time, her dress dried, and she walked back to the pool where their camp had been established.

Digger sat resting under a nearby tree, carving a piece of wood. Friz was nowhere to be seen. "Well," Digger said, "what did you find in the pool?"

She sat beside him. "I'm sorry about Horace, but he's so rude. I didn't realize my dress would go transparent. I think he did it deliberately."

"I didn't see anything."

"Horace was nasty."

"So, what's in there?"

"I don't know. It's another of those strange rooms with a lighted ceiling. There is a door and water coming up through the floor. There are also more dead people. The room must be inside that rock beside the pool."

"More dead people?"

"Yes. Friz says they're Japanese soldiers. I don't understand how they got there or why they're dead. The place looks new. Everything is so clean. And you can hear that horrible engine thing puffing away. I think someone lives there."

Digger stopped whittling, folded his knife and sat up, facing the girl. "No one lives there. It's just a cave."

"With electric light?"

"It's not electric light. Did you see a bulb?"

"No."

"Course not. It's luminescent rock. Probably miners built it hundreds of years ago. The Japs most likely died because they ran out of air hiding from the Americans."

"What about the engine? You can really hear it down there. It puffs and wheezes, real loud, it's scary, someone has look after it."

"I would think it's a natural sound made by the water dripping on something, probably a hot rock. Yes, that's what it is, just a geothermal sound effect."

"Well I don't know," she said softly and thoughtfully.

"Did Friz really see you; I mean did you show him your – well, did you?" Digger asked, displaying a little jealousy.

"What do you think?"

"I don't know, I didn't see anything."

"When I got out of the water in the cave room. I didn't realize my dress had turned transparent. So Friz took a good look before he said anything, then he was rude to me."

"I'll have a word with him. If we're going to survive here until they find us, we have to work together. We don't need to fight each other. You must agree there is something frightening on this island. What happened to the plane and all the dead bodies? I don't want you to frighten Friz though, he's only a kid."

"I don't know," she said. "There are dead people in all the caves, but there are none out here. Where did they go? Even Sandy vanished."

"I think you've hit it right on the head. Whatever took the plane is too big to fit in the caves. People died in the caves hiding from it."

THE ANDRILLA

Chapter 11

Before the sunset, Friz arrived back at camp with an old rusty rifle in his hands. Digger admonished him for collecting dangerous relics. The young boy remained adamant; it was his rifle – he found it. In the morning, Friz, as usual, awoke before the others. Quietly he splashed his face with the cold refreshing water from the limped pool and drank a little, then grabbed his old rifle and climbed the shallow cliff.

On top of the rocks, he found what looked like a highway that stretched into the distance. The almost perfectly smooth lava flow led right to the mountain in the centre of the island. Friz marched up the apparent road, pretending to be a Japanese soldier. Every now and again he would stop and shoot some of the enemy snipers who were hiding in the trees. The game finished when he reached the end of the highway near a vertical cliff face.

An almost inaccessible ledge led off to the left with a broad flat area beyond. Friz scrambled down. Its entire width was sprinkled with broken rocks. The energetic lad reached the plateau and stood at its edge to survey the jungle below. Sitting with his feet dangling over the cliff he pretended to shoot a few more enemy snipers hiding in the trees.

During his game, he spotted something interesting. Just

below his position on a rough outcrop of rocks nestled the entrance to a small cavern. It could be another cave filled with dead Japanese soldiers, he thought. Perhaps there would be a gun in good condition in there, maybe one that worked. Leaving his rifle on the plateau, he began the climb down. For a boy his age, the climb presented little difficulty and moments later he peered into a dark hole.

The cave was too small to stand in. Friz kneeled and slowly crawled into the tunnel. At length, he found a point where a considerable drop seemed to bar his progress. In the dark-gloomy cavern he could see nothing and this time no light magically come on to show the way. Carefully feeling his way, he found a step-down as his eyes were becoming accustomed to the gloom. The cave was dark and smelly and as far as he could determine, square.

Friz could hear his heart pounding in his chest mixed with the sound of machinery somewhere a long way off. This time it wasn't the dragon breathing, instead a whirring hum of smooth mechanical things. At a distance on the right the dark seemed total and impenetrable. Friz crept toward that area. It soon turned out to be a passage that led deep into the mountain. The walls were smooth, more like painted metal than rock.

Slowly and apprehensively, he crept along the dark tunnel until he reached its end. The sound of machinery became clear and there were small streams of light leaking in, about fifteen feet away on the left. Friz crept to the light and looked through one of the holes. Beyond in a brilliantly illuminated room lay strange-looking coffins standing in lines. It looked to him to be something out of a science fiction TV show.

A stationary fan and a flimsy grill stood between him and the room full of coffins. Climbing onto the sill he kicked the grill. It wasn't attached and fell freely out of the way. Horace clambered into the room. The freezing air made his breath steam. Most of the coffins were empty; two had sleeping or dead humans in them.

The large room had only one door, a stainless-steel device

with a frosted glass window. Gingerly, Horace pushed the door. It did not resist, swinging away easily it exposed yet a second one. He pushed his way through both sets and found himself standing at the head of a passageway about fifty or sixty feet long. Everything looked clean and new with no dust, dirt, or wreckage. The air smelled warm and sweet. To the right and to the left were more closed doors.

As he approached the entrance to his left, it silently slid open, revealing a room totally beyond the boy's comprehension. To him, it looked a bit like an X-ray centre at General Hospital. He stepped back and the door quietly closed. Approaching the door on the opposite side. It too, quietly and quickly opened revealing yet another room of mystery. He dared not enter. The room was filled with banks of push buttons and twinkling lights.

Mid-way down the hall he stopped at another doorway on the same side as the buttons and lights chamber. It, too, opened as he approached it. "Wow!" he said. "A TV room."

The room contained one comfortable looking armchair in front of a large TV screen. The area was dimly lit and at least fifteen by fifteen feet square, with nothing except a door on each of three walls and the screen on the fourth.

Horace felt the room to be friendlier and more inviting than any of the others. The TV was especially interesting. With a brief look up and down the corridor to check if anyone or thing was observing him, he slipped into the room. The portal silently closed behind him. Afraid of being trapped, he moved back to the entrance. It opened again. Somehow, the door sensed his presence.

Timidly, Horace walked to the large TV screen. As he approached, it came to life. A picture of some part of the island outdoors was displayed. Friz slumped into the easy chair. A voice said something in a foreign language. He jumped to his feet and looked around. The voice came from the TV.

Friz sat down once more. "I wish it was in English," he said. The voice came again "Why is your reflector not working?" Friz laughed. "Great, man! English, this is cool."

"Yes," the voice said. "English. Why is your reflector not working?"

"You're talking to me." He began to feel afraid.

"Do not be afraid, merely answer the question as presented."

"I don't know. What's a reflector?"

"Your identifier is not working properly. You must report to the medical room to have it replaced."

"Okay," Friz said. "Do you have any video games?"

"Video games, explain video games?"

"Yeah. Something to play on the TV."

The machine carefully analyzed the child's mind and located the source of the question. Instantly a replica of the Horace's broken game came to the screen. "Oh, cool," he said excitedly. "How can I play without a joystick or something?"

"Think your moves and I shall respond, for you."

True to its word, the wonderful machine played video games with the child for almost an hour, and then it demanded that he get his reflector repaired.

"Do I have to go?" Horace whined.

"It is essential for tracking. Were you on the air vehicle that I destroyed?"

"Was it you who shot us down?"

"Yes. For that, I am sorry. Your reflector was not detected until the vehicle crashed."

"Where is our plane now?" Horace said.

"It has been taken by the infestation."

"What about the dead men in those caves?"

"They are chambers, not caves. The infestation has not found them yet."

"What about those dead people in the cold room?"

"They are not dead. They are the creators. They are at rest, awaiting the return of the master. Now you must have your reflector repaired, then you may go anywhere you wish, and I will protect you."

"Okay. What do I have to do?"

"Go to the medical room and wait."

"Wait for what?" Friz said.

"The medical ambulator. It has been called the dragon's claw. Do not be afraid. It will help you not harm you."

"Who are you, Mister?"

"I am the Andrilla. The infestation calls me the dragon, for I am their enemy."

"Okay. Where is the medical room?"

"It was the first room you entered after the freeze chamber."

"Oh sure, I know." He jumped up and ran to the door, it opened automatically. The medical room door was already open. Friz felt happy, for now, he thought he knew all the answers. The others would really be surprised.

Once activated the medical room was awe-inspiring to the child. As he entered a voice spoke: "Stand in the circle."

Horace slowly walked to the designated spot. The huge cylinder thing attached to the ceiling came his way. It extended a claw-like robotic arm. The boy was gently lifted from the floor and placed on the examining table. The mechanical extension of the Andrilla carefully and gently examined him.

With surgical precision, the thing applied a local anaesthetic to his arm, cleaned it, sterilized the area and then injected the isotopic reflector. The whole thing was over in seconds. Although it offered no medical benefit, Friz felt better than he had for days. It was as if a load had been taken off his shoulders. Feeling more like a man than a child, he walked back to the control room and sat in the chair again.

"I've done it."

"You are free to go where you please. I shall lock the entrances that lead to the infestation for they are dangerous to us both."

"What is the infestation?"

"An evil force that has invaded our island. They must be destroyed."

"Great, I'll help," Friz said. He got up and began his exploration. Farther down the passage on the right-hand side he found another door. It opened as he approached. Beyond was a half circle of stairs that led into a long room with water running down one side in a channel.

Friz entered the room. At the far end he found another portal with a luminescent opening panel. The water dropped through a hole in the floor. Pressing the panel he opened the door. About five steps down there was another almost identical chamber. Water came up through the floor and flowed down a channel to the end of the room where it dropped through the floor again. About halfway down, on the right-hand side he found another door.

Curiosity led the boy to the middle door. He pressed the panel. Silently, the entrance opened. The sound of machinery became very loud. Entering the room he found that the temperature was at least ten degrees hotter. The thump and wheeze of the dragon seemed loud and frightening. Quickly, he exited the chamber and ran all the way back to the half-circle of stairs, up the stairs and back into the friendly familiar corridor. There were still two other doors not examined.

The first was an incomprehensible room filled with desks and controls. "Mission control." Friz said. He tried the second. A large staircase led up to another entrance well above ceiling level. Placing his hand on the panel, he opened the door. Friz's eyes almost expanded to the size of saucers when he saw what was beyond the door. A gigantic room with an immense golden robot either side of the doorway.

The two huge golden robots were standing silent guard over the empty room. Each had a red and a blue curly hose leading to their navels. "Wow!" Friz said as he felt the smoothness of the fifteen-foot figure. Thoroughly happy and excited, he ran back to the Andrilla and sat in the seat.

"This is a cool place. You're my best friend. I'd like to stay here."

"You are welcome to do as you wish. There is no food for biological creatures here."

"What's the two terror bots for?"

Reading his mind the machine answered: "They are guardians of the Andrilla."

"How do I get back to my friends on the beach?"

"You cannot leave. The infestation is between you and the exit."

"Why do some of the doors have that shiny panel to open them, and some don't?"

"They are for the destruction of any infestation."

"How's that work?"

"Any infestation in the outer limits will not be indicated therefore unknown to me. Should they touch the panel, the automatic defence system will be activated if they do not have a reflector."

"What's that mean?"

"They will be destroyed."

Friz had been with the Andrilla for hours and he had become famished. Reluctantly, he walked back through the cold room, climbed through the vent and then through the passage to the outside world. He reasoned that it may be faster to use the pool as an exit but this time he chose the scary route. It was late afternoon when, hungry and happy, Horace reached the limpid pool.

"Where have you been?" Lizzie shouted.

Horace climbed down the cliff face and confronted the girl. "I've been with the Andrilla."

"You've been with Ann who?"

"Andrilla. I know what happened to the airplane."

Lizzie didn't know just how to react to the kid. "Well, don't keep us in suspense, genius."

"The Andrilla said that the infestation ate it."

"Sure," Lizzie said in disbelief.

"It's true. I've met the Dragon of Hope Island."

Digger was slightly old-fashioned. He didn't like lying or gross exaggeration. "I don't want to hear about your imaginary exploits."

"It's not imagination," Friz said. "I talked to Andrilla. He told me all about the infestation. How it consumes everything. It didn't eat the dead Japanese because it didn't know they were there."

"Give it up, Friz. I don't want to know."

"I can prove it to you. I've been there. You wouldn't believe what I've seen, honest."

"What if he's telling the truth?" Lizzie said.

"He's not. I would rather not hear anymore about it."

"I'll show you, Liz. If you'll come with me, I'll show you. You can talk to Andrilla, just like I did."

"Okay," she said. "I'll come."

"Great. All we got to do is drop in through the pool."

"You little pervert," she said. "You just want my dress to turn transparent again."

He was mortally wounded by the incorrect assumption. "Alright, fatty. You don't have to come, why should I care."

"I'm going to kill that kid," she said as though talking to some unseen person.

"I'll come with you Friz," Digger said. "If you stop bugging Elizabeth."

"Great, Digger. I promise."

"But not today, we'll go first thing in the morning. Now I want you to give Elizabeth her necklace back."

"Why?"

"Because it's hers."

"Sure, if you say so." He put his hand in his pocket and pulled out the necklace. "Here, Lizzie, this is yours. I repaired the clasp. You bent it when you ripped it off. Are we friends now?"

"No," she said. "I don't want it. It's from my father. I don't want anything to do with him. He hasn't even missed me yet, I hate him."

Digger tried to make peace saying: "It is yours, Lizzie. You should keep it. It's probably valuable."

"No," she said firmly. "I'll give it to you. Here." She snatched it from Horace and handed it to Digger. "To you with love from me."

Digger took the pendant and placed it around his neck. It was the first present he had ever received from a girl. "I'll look after it for you. I'm sure you'll want it back when we are rescued."

Horace felt happy that someone believed him. Quickly, he got stuck into a coconut; it was his first piece of food for the day. The night passed quietly except for the breathing of the dragon. Horace no longer worried about the strange sound. He knew it was friendly. Again in the morning, he was the first to awaken, and ran off searching for breakfast.

DRAGON FIRE

Chapter 12

On tropical islands, the mornings are damp, usually starting with a mist raised by the heat of the early sun. The condition lasts only thirty minutes or so before the tropical heat dispels the fog. Horace enjoyed the morning inversion, it sent chills through his body and galvanized him, acting almost like an alarm clock. Without a care or thought he danced off into the jungle.

Unlike most children of his age, Horace was bright, observant, and daring. His foray into the jungle quickly rewarded him with the finding of a rambutan tree, the fruit of which is sweet, nutritious and filling. Collecting several twigs loaded with the prickly fruit he returned to camp. "Here," he said. "Lichee for everyone."

The fruit is sweet and squishy, once the chestnut-like husk is removed. After breakfast, Horace asked when they would visit the Andrilla.

"Is there really such a thing?" Digger said.

"If you come, I'll show you."

"No silly tricks?"

"Honest, Digger, no tricks, silly or otherwise."

"So how do we do it?"

"Well, for a non-swimmer, it's difficult, but the shortest

route is right here. All we got to do is get to the bottom of the pool and up the other side. It's only bobbing down and jumping up the other side. It really is easy. Lizzie did it. I'll help you, you won't have any trouble, all you have to do is hold your breath for a few seconds."

The fear of water began to show on Digger's face. "I don't know if I can do it, Friz. I can't swim, you know."

"Sure you can. We'll take it nice and slow."

The two took off their shoes and shirts. Friz slipped into the water. "Come on, Digger. There's nothing to fear, I promise."

Digger clung tightly to the bank and slipped into the cold water. "I'm ready," he said, his voice trembling.

"Take a deep breath." Friz said. "Hold my hand, and I'll lead you down. Okay?"

"Okay." Digger took a deep breath. Holding hands, the two attempted to dive below the water. The dive was a failure. Digger panicked and scrambled for the surface. His flailing, almost drowning Horace.

"Not to worry," Horace said, spluttering back to the surface. "We'll try again. Just hold your breath and trust me. I won't let anything happen to you."

After a few seconds, the pair were ready to try again. A deep breath and down they went. Horace dragged his struggling friend into the tunnel, and in seconds they surfaced. Digger, excited and frightened, struggled frantically for the edge of the pool. He rubbed the water from his eyes as he clung on for dear life. The two slowly climbed from the water and into the brightly lit chamber.

"Holy smoke!" Digger said, looking around the room. "Who owns this place?"

"The Andrilla. Don't touch those luminous panels on the doors"!

"Why?"

"The Andrilla said that the panel is the thing that starts the automatic defence. If you touch it, you will be killed instantly. But I'm okay."

"Oh, why are you so great?" Digger said.

"I've been reflected, so the Andrilla knows me. You haven't, so it won't know you. Don't touch anything, okay?"

"Sure. I'm freezing. It's awful cold in here."

"Come on," Horace said encouragingly. "It's a lot warmer up here." Quickly he pressed the panel and the door slid aside. "Come on. I'll show you where the dragon lives."

Amazement showed on Digger's face as they entered the strange place. Although the rooms all looked alike, it was still wondrous. Friz quickly and excitedly ran the length of the room and pressed the next panel. He stood in the doorway waiting for Digger to catch him up. "That's the door to hell," he said, trying to frighten his companion.

Quickly, Horace pressed the panel to open the door to the geothermal reactor room. The wheezing of the dragon became very loud. Heat wafted through the open door. Digger's eyes were wide as he peered into the immense chamber. "I don't believe it. I've never seen the like. What on earth is it?"

Friz's eyes flashed wild excitement. At last, he had achieved something. Digger had to believe him now. "I would like to show this place to my mum and dad. It's really cool."

"I'm sorry about your parents, Friz, but look on the bright side."

"Bright side?"

"They are probably looking down now and are proud of their son."

"Yeah. Just wait until you meet Andrilla. I've played video games with him. He knows everything in the world."

"Sure, Friz, whatever you say," Digger said, still in disbelief.

They walked deeper into the remarkable new world. Everything was as if in a dream, engines of strange and monstrous power. They crossed a gantry of shining clean metal and below it ran a river of pure molten magma. It shimmered as it moved slowly on its way. The dragon itself turned out to be a weird and wonderful device, like a beam engine. With a beam of more than a hundred feet long it slowly worked, pumping up and down, hissing and wheezing.

The works of the magnificent beam were not obvious, but it shimmered as if it too were red-hot. Steam occasionally hissed from unseen cylinders. Great quantities of water were diverted to some huge underground river. The water moved slowly and majestically, almost undisturbed. It's clarity, was such that the bottom of the river could be seen clearly through it.

"We should be getting back, Friz," Digger suddenly said.

"You haven't met the Andrilla yet. Just meet him, then we'll go."

"No. We can't leave Lizzie too long on her own, she's only a girl, you know. We have to look after her."

"Ah!" Friz moaned. "She always spoils everything. I hate sheilas."

"Come on, Friz, don't be a spoiled brat. We'll come back later and do some more exploring. Besides that, I'm getting hungry."

"How about just one quick look at the Andrilla?"

"Hurry then. I'm worried about Lizzie."

Excitedly, Horace led the way. He ran ahead, then ran back to encourage the slow Digger. "Come on, we're wasting time."

Eventually, they reached the circular stairs where the water welled up through the floor. Digger stopped to examine the chamber and the water. "I wonder what it's for?"

"What?"

"The water. Why does the water come up through the floor like that, and where does it go?"

"Don't know. Who cares? Come on, the best bit's just up here." Horace opened the door and waited for Digger to climb the steps.

Together, they entered the corridor. Digger's eyes were wide and staring. "I don't understand this place. What is it? Who built it?"

"Come on, in this room." Horace was jumping up and down with the excitement of sharing his knowledge with a friend.

Digger slowly and cautiously advanced. His mind was having difficulty absorbing the strangeness. He drew his breath in sharply as he observed the Andrilla room. "We can't go in there."

"Sure we can." Horace leapt into the control seat. "Hi, Andrilla. I've brought you a visitor."

"The visitor has a faulty reflector." The Andrilla said.

Digger refused to enter the room, standing by the open door. The hidden source of the voice inspired him with fear. "Come on Friz, we've got to get out of here. I don't like it."

"Just one go. You'll love it. It plays any video game you can think of."

"Friz. Come on. This place is dangerous. Let's go. Now."

Reluctantly, Horace climbed from the seat. "Goodbye Andrilla. I'll come back."

The machine did not reply. Digger had already made his way down the circular stairs – he wanted to get out of the place. "Come on Friz. We've got to get back to Lizzie. She'll be terribly worried about us."

"You'll come back with me tomorrow?"

"Sure, Friz. I'd love to."

The two carefully retraced their steps to the limpid pool chamber where the dead Japanese soldiers lay undisturbed.

"A thing called the sting killed them both, "Friz said. "It won't hurt us, 'cuz I've been reflected. We should get you reflected, then the Andrilla will protect you, too. See how it said your reflection was broken too."

THE INFESTATION SPREADS

Chapter 13

Morning brought yet another clear and rainless day. The heat shimmered over the empty turquoise ocean. Still, there were no rescue planes or ships. Lizzie and Digger sat on the silver sand at the ocean's edge.

"I think they've forgotten us," Elizabeth said sadly. "We're marooned forever."

"I don't understand," Digger replied. "They've had plenty of time. They must have a clue to where we are. The sky should be filled with search planes."

"It has to be my father. He's the only person who could call off the search. It's the perfect way to get rid of me. I hate him. If we ever get back to civilization, I'll never speak to him again."

"I've been thinking," Digger said, lying flat on his back. "The real shipping lanes are west of here. We should build a boat or a raft and get off this island before Horace's infestation catches up with us."

"Do you believe in his Andrilla thing?"

"Not really. He's found some ancient mining engine and a control room. It looks like it still works, or at least it's moving. The poor kid dreams a lot, an' he's lonely, so he invents all these stories with just the tiniest hint of reality. The control room has some kind of automatic voice thing. You talk to it, and it talks back, but it doesn't do anything."

"Look!" Lizzie yelled jumping to her feet. She pointed to the horizon.

Digger looked in disbelief. For the first time since they had arrived, a ship could be seen in the distance. "It's very far away, but it is a ship. We've got to signal it before it's out of range. We should have built a signal beacon. What are we going to do?"

"We've got to get the flare gun. It's at the limpid pool." Elizabeth gasped and began to run.

Digger ran after her, across the headlands, across the pampas grass, and through the woods to the clearing where the limpid pool nestled beneath the cliffs. Grabbing the little suitcase, they began the long return journey. Breathlessly, they arrived at the beach.

"Where's the ship?" Digger said scanning the horizon and shading his eyes.

"There, there!" she yelled excitedly.

As quickly as possible, Lizzie took out the pistol, snapped open the breach and put in one of the two cartridges. She pointed it skyward and pulled the trigger. With a bang, the brilliant white flare rushed hundreds of feet upwards, arced and came down crashing into the sea.

"Did they spot it?" Digger said bouncing up and down with excitement.

"I don't know," she said, ejecting the spent flare and reloading she pointed the gun skyward again.

"Fire!" Digger shouted. "Fire, fire!"

"No," she said sadly and lowered the gun. "There's no point, they're too far away. We'll never be rescued. We'll be here the rest of our lives." Tears began to trickle down her face.

"Don't cry, Lizzie. There'll be other ships and closer next time. You see if I'm not right."

She thumped down onto the beach and sat cross-legged, tears still trickling down her face. "Stupid dingoes. I hate them all."

Digger sat beside her. "Don't let it get you down. We'll be rescued, I promise."

"How can you promise that?"

He stroked her hair. "We'll be okay. You'll see. We'll start building a raft today so we can get away from this island get closer to the shipping lanes."

Lizzie slumped backwards and lay flat out on the sand. "Do you have a girlfriend, Digger?"

"No."

"Can I be your girl?"

"You are. You have been since we got here."

"Do you think I'm fat?"

"Well, you are, sort of. Well, sort of nicely rounded," he said trying to be diplomatic.

"Do you think I'm pretty, Digger?"

Digger felt awkward. The girl was a dumpling, a friend, a pal but nothing more. "I like you, Lizzie, you're nice, very nice."

Horace had been playing with the Andrilla, a grand and complicated video game, then eventually became hungry and decided to leave the mountain-dragon in search of food. For a change, he decided to leave via the freezing room, through the air vent and onto the plateau. As he began the long walk back to the limped pool he spotted the flare. He didn't really want to be rescued. He was happy living with the Andrilla.

"Stupid sheila," he shouted, "we got no school, no stupid grownups, and she wants to leave."

Finding lunch presented no problem. There were many trees that bore fruit, mango, papaya, passion fruit, coconut, and the bananas were just coming into season. Arriving at the pool Horace looked around; the place was deserted. He put his lunch down near the fresh water, sat down and began his meal.

Lizzie and Digger, disappointed that they were unable to attract the attention of the ship, decided to return to the limpid pool. Hand-in-hand, they walked back. Halfway across the pampas grass, Digger spun and fell to the ground. As he fell a bang echoed in the distance. The boy lay on his back, an expression of surprise on his face. Elizabeth knelt down to help him.

Confusion and alarm showed clearly in the girl's eyes "Digger, what's wrong?" She put one arm under him in an attempt to lift him. "Digger, what's wrong with you?"

The boy smiled sickly; his eyes rolled in his head a tremor shook his body violently. "Keep this," he said, holding out his hand.

Lizzie took the necklace. "Digger, get up. We have to go; we've got to leave this place. Stop messing about."

"I feel cold, Lizzie. I feel cold. I love you. I'm sorry I said you were fat. I didn't mean it." He closed his eyes and went limp.

Lizzie pulled the boy to her. The terrible cold reality of what had happened filtered through to her confused mind. She suddenly heard footfalls heading her way. With a sudden and angry urge she pulled out the flare gun and stood to face the oncoming foe. A surprised Chinese soldier stopped in his tracks only yards away. Calmly, she raised her arm and fired. The white-hot flare struck the soldier square in the chest. He screamed and staggered. In seconds, the magnesium fumes, burning nylon, and flesh brought him to his knees.

Lizzie knelt down beside her friend. "I've killed the bastard," she whispered, and then struggled to raise the dead boy. "Come on, Digger. We've got to get out of here." As she struggled, he rolled over and fell on his face. Lizzie screamed at the terrible damage to the boy's back. Leaping to her feet she began to run in sheer terror and blind panic. As the girl ran, she heard the sound of angry bees scream by her ears.

Lizzie ran across the grass and through the trees, Friz stood as if waiting for her. "What's all the noise?" he said in surprise.

"Run, Friz. They killed Digger. They're after us." Again she heard the sound like angry bees rushing by. Some struck the rock face and burst into pieces, some whined off into the distance.

"Quick, into the pool," Friz yelled.

They held hands and ran to the pool. More angry bees flew by and one stung Lizzie in the chest. They reached the pool and leaped into the cold water. As they reached the other side and began climbing from the pond, the girl felt dizzy. Friz climbed from the pool. "Come on, Liz. Come on. The Andrilla will protect us. Hurry."

The boy's voice seemed to be in the distance. The world had begun to take on an unreal appearance. His words slowly made no sense. Friz turned to look at her, his face aghast. She looked down following his stare. The front of her transparent dress was bright red and the red reached the floor, even the floor began turning red.

Quickly Friz hit the panel. The door opened and he stood in the doorway. "Come on, Lizzie. Quick, come on. The infestation is coming."

She staggered forward, and the world slowly began to melt before her eyes. Painfully and tearfully, she staggered past the lad in the doorway. As Friz stepped back to allow the door to close, he saw hands reaching up out of the limpid pool. The door closed and Lizzie fell to the ground. "Andrilla," Horace screamed. "Andrilla, help me." Tears of fear and excitement flooded down his face, he bounced on the spot in near uncontrolled fear.

Suddenly, he heard the unmistakable crack of the dragon sting, and again. "Yes," Friz yelled, demonstrating his joy with a powerful uppercut in thin air. "Yes, die you dingoes." He put his hand on the panel. Silently, the door slid open revealing two fresh wet and smoking bodies. Next, he turned to the girl. She was still breathing but not moving.

"Come on, Lizzie. You'll be all right. Come on."

She did not respond to the boy's encouragement. Her limp body lay in an ever-growing pool of blood mixed with water. Suddenly, in fear, he leaped up realizing that now he was truly alone in the world. No parents, no Digger, and no Lizzie. He ran crying to the only comfort he knew. Through the long rooms passed the geothermal reactor and to the Andrilla control centre.

"Andrilla, Andrilla!" He screamed leaping onto the chair. "You must help me, Andrilla!"

"Calm yourself. We shall solve all problems. The infestation chased you. They have been destroyed."

"It's Lizzie, Elizabeth. She's bleeding really bad. You've got to help me, she'll die."

The calm and patient voice answered: "Take her to the medical room. The dragon's talon will repair her."

"She's too heavy. I can't do it; you've got to help me." Tears rushed down his face.

"There is a wheeled vehicle in the deep sleep chamber. The cold room, it is in the wall closet at the end of the room. Enter, turn right and it is at the end. Use it to bring the Lizzie to the medical room."

"Okay, okay." Beginning to regain control, Friz ran to the cold chamber, through the double set of doors, turned right and then ran to the end of the room. Sure enough, there he found a closet and, in the closet, a wheeled stretcher standing on end. It was a low vehicle, with wheels only the size of skate wheels, though it would work admirably well for his purpose.

Quickly as possible, he dragged the device out of the room, up the corridor, and to the half-round staircase. Bungling the trolley through the door and down the steps was difficult, yet he did it. Running with the truck in tow, he rushed through the four long water rooms to where Lizzie still lay motionless on the ground.

He parked the vehicle beside her and then with all his might tried to roll the dead weight of her body onto the small flatbed. After some considerable struggling, he managed to get her on her back and onto the trolley. He ran as fast as he could, dragging the vehicle behind him. Although there were only seven steps, it represented a terrible obstacle to Horace. He tightened the straps on the buggy to hold the girl firmly to the vehicle over the rough terrain.

Climbing the steps and dragging the girl as best he could

behind him, he reached the top almost exhausted. The door opened, and he dragged her through to the next chamber. He eventually reached the half-round staircase. There was no way a boy, so small, could drag the trolley up those steps. Friz began to cry again, panic flooding his veins. Fearfully, he listened to see if she was still breathing. Her dress now completely soaked in blood. The trolley was soaked in blood and even Friz had become red with the girl's life essence.

Unstrapping the girl he pulled her by her the arms, dragged the limp body up the stairs, leaving a trail of crimson. Opening the door and dragging her slowly and blindly into the corridor, then rushing back to gather the trolley. Tears blurring his vision he began climbing the circular stairs. With a sudden slip on the fresh blood he let go of the trolley. Noisily the vehicle bumped down the steps, rolled across the floor and plunged into the well, vanishing from sight. Though every muscle in his body ached he dragged the girl down the corridor and at last reached the circle on the medical room floor.

"Help me," he cried and stepped back trembling, hoping the dragon would do its thing and save the girl.

A great feeling of relief, almost peace came over him as the fearful looking talon approached the silent, blood-soaked teenager. Gracefully, the robotic extension of the Andrilla's psyche picked the girl up and began its examination of the damage. Friz slumped against the door frame and started crying in open relief. The terrible strain and responsibility had come to an end, now it was the turn of the machine to show just how clever it really could be.

The mechanical device quickly and accurately removed the girl's clothing, destroying them in the process. Its penetrating eyes quickly assessed the situation and the operation began. Friz slowly walked to the control room and sat in the magic seat, almost totally drained of energy.

"You have done well," the Andrilla said softly. "The girl is dying. She has lost so much body fluid; her brain will soon die."

"You've got to help her," Friz screamed excitedly.

"It is possible. You must return to the medical room. Stand on the special spot."

"Why?"

"The girl needs your assistance."

Frightened by the prospect that he may be the last living human on the island, Friz walked the blood-soaked corridor to the medical room. The place looked like a slaughterhouse. The floor was soaked in the girl's dark and congealing blood. Even the walls and doors had blood where Friz had stopped or leaned. His hands and clothes were dark red and caked in the crimson goo.

He stood on the appointed spot and looked around the weird room. Lizzie was lying still and deathly grey, completely naked, on the workbench of the talon. A second table had mysteriously put itself next to Lizzie. The talon silently sped across the ceiling and stopped before Friz. Gently, it supported his back, captured him and lifted him to the spare table.

Horace was unable to move, all limbs pinioned as the talon began its mysterious work. Quickly it cleaned and sterilized an area on the boy's arm. Some form of pain killing anaesthetic was applied. Blood began to flow up the tube that the machine attached to his arm. Clear fluid began to flow down another tube to the girl's arm. While he lay unable to move, the strange machine cleaned the lad and removed his filthy clothing. Sleep overcame him as he reclined in welcome relief.

CAPTURED

Chapter 14

When he eventually awoke, Horace found himself covered by a clean white cloth. Lizzie had been treated likewise. The thing with the giant eyes still hovered around apparently examining its handiwork. The machine instantly recognized that he had regained consciousness. It released the clamps, freeing all his limbs. The tubing had already been removed, both from him and the girl. Lizzie lay motionless with new tubing in her other arm. As Friz climbed from the table the talon brought him a pair of overalls. He felt very dizzy and weak.

Bashful of the unconscious girl, Friz climbed into the suit. The blood-soaked remnants of her clothes were on a shelf beneath her. The boy stepped close. Her necklace lay on top of the heap. Admiring it, he took and put it around his own neck. "I'll give it back when you can walk," he said and left the room. The corridor was still bloodstained. He entered the control room and sat on the seat. "Andrilla, how is Elizabeth?"

"The girl is alive, though there is bad news."

"What's the bad news, Andrilla?"

"The infestation has broken into the chamber of the guardians."

"Where?"

"The room where you saw what you call the Terror bots."

"So, kill them all."

"There is one who is like you. He leads the infestation on their quest of destruction. You must stop them."

"Me?" Horace said shocked. "How can I stop the infestation?"

"Start the guardians for me. The masters cannot help. You will have to do it all by yourself."

"How?"

"Enter the chamber of the guardians and remove the mute and null lines from them. They will awaken and destroy the infestation."

"How do I do that?"

"There are two coiled tubes attached to each of the guardians a red one and a blue one. You must remove both red ones. One from each guardian, then remove both blue ones."

"And that'll fix the infestation?"

"Yes, it will also be the end. Will *you* do it?"

"Sure. The end of what?"

"First you must obtain food for the girl, she cannot travel without food. Give it to the Talon. It will process the food and feed her. After activation, you must leave."

The feeling of dizziness had passed, though still the feeling of loneliness persisted. He desperately wanted to speak with the girl. What had happened to Digger was still a mystery. The lonely boy, now frightened almost of his own shadow, left the complex through the air vent in the cold room. Once outside, he felt that even the trees were watching him. The air was filled with sounds he had never noticed before.

As quickly as possible, he collected fallen coconuts, and a handful of rambutans. With breath drawn in gulps, he scuttled back to the vent into the safety of the Andrilla. He placed the food in the circle for the Talon to collect. Elizabeth remained still and quiet. Friz walked over to her and held her hand.

"I'm sorry I was mean to you." She did not respond. The girl lay still and grey, her expression peaceful. "I'm now going to save us all. I have to go kill the infestation. The ones that hurt you are dead and rotting in the pool chamber. I love you, Lizzie. You're the only person I have left in the world. Please get better."

Carefully, he placed the girl's hand back on her stomach, and brushed the tears from his eyes. As he turned and left, her eyes opened and watched him leave. The door closed; Friz felt terrified. The Andrilla had said that it would be the end. Again brushing the tears from his eyes, he walked to the end of the corridor, opened the door, and climbed the long staircase.

He knew there was terror on the other side of the last door. As he approached, he heard the crack of the dragon's sting. Suddenly, the impulse took him and he ran the last few steps. The door opened. He stood face to face with an Asian looking gentleman. The man grabbed him just as all hell broke loose. Desperately he struggled to escape, but the man was strong.

The room filled with smoke, explosion after explosion. Pieces of shrapnel rained down. Crack after crack, the sting slaughtered the unseen foe. The man holding Horace ran through the hellfire to the other end of the room. There, he pressed the panel, and soon they were alone in the giant elevator. Peter put the boy down. "You're safe here son."

"You dingo," Friz yelled. "I'll kill the lot of you." He kicked Peter on the shin, just as the elevator door opened. Like a shot he was off, running in the great hangar where his plane wreckage was stored.

The Chinese guards quickly caught him, knocking him to the floor with a rifle butt. Friz lay silent, unconscious, and bleeding. Peter ran to the boy's assistance. He did not know the language of the guards, and before he could affect a rescue, they knocked him senseless to the floor.

Some time passed before Peter awoke. The battle for the chamber of the Guardians had reached its conclusion. Both stings were destroyed at a cost of seven lives. Work began immediately on the door that Friz had come through. The two golden idols seemed impervious to any attempt to cut them. Thermal lance, or acetylene torch, had no effect. For fear of creating some unknown chain reaction the curly tube-like wires in the idol's navel were left alone.

Peter was ordered to examine the idols and make his recommendations. "Where is the boy?" he demanded.

Arjit had never seen the lad, but he translated the question to the leader and back. "He says the boy will be tortured until he either tells what we want to know or dies of his injuries."

"For heaven's sake, Arjit." Peter said. "Make them understand that the kid doesn't know Korean or Chinese. I can talk to him. Make them let me talk to him. I'll find out what they want."

"He says no?" Arjit said.

"Tell him I won't work here wasting my time when I can get all I need from the kid. Make him understand."

Again Arjit put forward the argument. "He says okay, you have thirty minutes. If you get nothing, the kid will die."

"Okay, alright. I'll do whatever they want. Let's get to the boy."

They were led to one of the offices off the long corridor. The place was full of guards. Peter and Arjit were led into the room. They found Horace tied to an office chair in the middle of the floor.

"Hi, son," Peter said softly.

"Oh! The dickhead that speaks English," Friz said hatefully.

"I'm here to help you, son."

"You're the stupid dingo that stopped me."

"I've been given half an hour to help you, boy. If you don't help me, we'll both die, is that what you want?"

"Good. You'll never beat the Andrilla. It'll kill the lot of you. I know, because it told me so."

"Andrilla? What's an Andrilla?"

"It's the Dragon of Hope Island. It knows you. You're the leader of the infestation." Friz spat at Peter. "I hope you drown in vomit with all these other pigs. You wait until the Andrilla gets you."

"Please, son, I'm in the same situation you are. I would

rather not be in this place. I'm as much a prisoner as you are."

"You're a reflector?" Friz said brightening up.

"I don't know what you're talking about, kid, but these people don't mess about. Both you and I will die in less than half an hour if you don't help me."

"Help you what?" Friz said.

"I have to give these people something they'll believe about this place. Tell me about this place. What is it?"

"I'll tell you nothing."

"Listen, son," Peter said raising his voice. "I don't want to die. Please just talk to us. Maybe together we can escape."

"Get stuffed," he shouted and spat again.

A guard punched the child in the face. Blood flushed down the boy's nose. Peter leapt up. "Stop it, you stupid bastard." The guard thumped him in the chest with his rifle butt. Peter groaned. "Please help us, boy, before it's too late."

The lights went out, casting everyone in total darkness. After some seconds, Friz spoke up. "I can get the lights back on," he said softly.

Arjit translated to the guards. Orders were given and in less than three minutes, some people came running with hand-held electric light.

GOLDEN TERROR

Chapter 15

Friz tried hard not to cry though the pain in his face was severe.

"They say the boy must remain restrained," Arjit said.

"I'm not concerned with what they say, if they want the light and air-conditioning back, they better do as I tell them," Peter snarled.

Arjit translated. There was considerable haggling, with arm waving and raised voices. "They say if the boy is to be freed, they have to break his leg to stop him running away. It is that, or they kill him here and now."

Peter knew that they would act like automatons and shoot before asking questions. "No let me take the boy, I'll guard him."

"The commander says no the boy is too dangerous."

"I'll agree to restraints then. But I want them to promise that no harm will come to the lad if he can get the power back."

Again Arjit argued with the head of the guards. The darkness and slowly fouling air frightened them. They were ready to agree with provisions.

"What do they want, Arjit?"

"The boy will tell you what to do, you will do it. If the lights do not come back, then … Then …"

"Yes?" Peter said.

"Then they will kill you and the child." Arjit said stroking the boy's head. Suddenly, he spotted the necklace around Horace's neck. Carefully and gently he took it from the lad.

"Give it back," Horace shouted angrily.

Peter looked at the boy. "Did you hear that; they'll kill both of us? These people don't mess about."

"Andrilla will kill them all just for being here. Now give me back the necklace, or I won't help you."

"Show me how to get the power back, and then we'll think about the necklace, alright?"

"No, you can all die of poison air. Why should I care?"

Arjit translated what the boy said to the head of the guards. Another argument broke out, again much arm flapping. "They want the boy tied to you, with a rope around his neck and his hands tied behind his back. This is the only way, or they shoot him now."

"Will you go for that boy?" Peter said.

"If the Indian comes with us," Horace said changing his tactics.

Again Arjit explained and several heads nodded. It was agreed that the boy should be tethered to Peter and that Arjit would be with them. The boy was tied to Peter on a short lead, with his hands restrained firmly behind his back. The complex had a ghostly quality without the white lights and clean smelling fresh air.

The armed crowd made its way to the big room, then up the stairs, along the passage and into the guardian chamber. The room was a ghastly glimpse of hell. Black smudges on the ceiling, bloodstains on the floor, wreckage, and pieces all around. Horace's terror bots stood as they had for centuries, motionless and as imposing as ever.

"Well?" Peter said. "What do we do now?"

Horace's eyes glistened with hatred "Let me go and I'll tell you. You're all going to die anyway."

"You know the deal, boy. Do it now or they'll shoot us both.

So how do we get in?"

"Get in where?"

"Through the door away from these guards."

"We don't get in, you've got to pull out those plugs, and in the right order. There's a special order."

"What plugs?"

Horace nodded his head towards one of the idols. "You must pull out the red ones first. One from each ... thing."

"Why?"

"Do you want the lights back on, or what?"

"You do it, Arjit," Peter said. "I'll guard the kid."

Arjit walked to the first Guardian, reached up and pulled out the red lead. It was some form of electrical plug. He walked over to the other and pulled out the red line. Nothing happened, the lights remained out, and the air-conditioning still did not operate.

"Now the blue ones," Horace said quietly. He pulled on the rope to get closer to the door between the two guardians.

Arjit pulled the last-coloured line from one of the golden idols with no response. He walked over to the second and pulled the line free. Everyone stood with bated breath. Suddenly, the lights came on. The sound of machinery rumbled in the distance as the air-conditioning started up. Peter smiled. Now at least their lives would be spared, for the moment. Suddenly, one of the guardians made a sound, like a small motor whirring. Everyone looked at the golden idol in horror.

An iris opened in the centre of what would be its forehead. Inside it looked like a raging furnace. The second guardian did likewise. All eyes were on them, fearful of the imminent and unknown danger. Suddenly, the door between them opened and Horace tried to enter. A red beam of light shot from the iris in one of the guardians. The destructive beam cut down the Chinese troops like a scythe. Some attempted to return fire. The second guardian vaporized anything that resisted.

Quickly of inspiration and fear, Peter pushed Arjit and the boy through the open door. It closed behind them. The two guardians were indeed robots of terrible power created from a technology centuries ahead of Earth's. Though no joints were visible, the giants began to move menacingly. One walked towards the great lift or elevator, the other to the corridor where some troops were skulking.

The carnage was terrible and complete. The ray from the head of the monsters devastated anything it touched. Blasting great holes in the walls and the almost indestructible door melted on contact. The elevator opened and one robot entered. Then the door closed. Total panic enveloped the armed guards all over the complex. As quickly as possible, they tried to find somewhere to hide from the monsters. The elevator stopped and the door opened.

Two quick laser blasts crushed the feeble resistance. The machine then destroyed the door to the outside world. It was blown away like tinsel. Slowly and deliberately, the guardian advanced to the great outdoors. The terrible laser cracking occasionally, evaporating any and all in its path. As the golden marvel moved out onto the beach, the *Miasaki II* came into its view way out on the ocean.

The massive robot stood for a few seconds as if trying to weigh the situation in its mind. Then, with unbelievable power, the laser reached out over the mile or so of ocean and destroyed a powerboat on its way to the *Miasaki II*. A great black mushroom cloud of burning diesel oil billowed up into the clear blue sky. The Guardian was intent on revenge over every part of the infestation.

The great robot slowly, made its way north along the beach, burning, killing, and destroying like the scythe of the angel of death. As though beckoned by some unseen force, it sought out all opposition. It plodded north menacingly. Suddenly, there came the scream of artillery and explosions a quarter of a mile inland. The second salvo struck the beach, showering the golden monster with sand and debris. The robot stopped and turned to face the sea as though trying to observe the origin.

The shells started to come in a steady rain. Someone on the

island was calling in the artillery and spotting the fall. The ship-based gun corrected its aim with every shot. One round landed at the guardian's feet. The monster crashed to the earth. Another shell struck near its head. Undamaged and undaunted the indestructible machine climbed to its feet and began walking toward the sea. Unexpectedly, the white light of the mountain weapon lashed out over the open water.

The submarine was about five miles out, resting in the calm water. The deck gun was rapidly firing, following the orders of someone on the conning tower. The white light of the mountain laser struck the deck gun causing the unspent ammunition to explode. The second strike hit the conning tower, sending cascades of hot metal into the sea. Bodies and fragments of the ancient vessel fell into the water.

The alarm sounded, and the sub began an emergency dive in an attempt to escape the mountain's laser. The golden Guardian knew that the threat had been taken care of and resumed its sweep along the beach. No one fired. Only the crashing of the giant's feet broke the silence. Rocks forced the Guardian inland, yet still, its quest was the northerly most point of the island.

As the monster broke through the trees, it found a clearing with a tent. Twenty people were hiding in the vicinity and eighteen with their weapons pointing at the golden intruder.

"Don't shoot," shouted someone.

The guardian had completed its quest by beating a path to the camp of the intruders. It stopped and waited for its companion to catch up. The battle for Dragon's Nest Island was all but complete, few if any of the Chinese troops still lived.

SATELLITE MADECCA

Chapter 16

Peter Chan had left with Sammy for a planned day on the town an hour or so ago when Mr. Enright called on his intercom: "Please come into my office, Miss Yan."

The pretty Eurasian girl came through the great oak door. "Yes sir?"

The jolly-overweight man sat at his desk. He stroked his pate in thoughtful contemplation. "Oh good! My daughter will be coming here for her annual school holiday, this time I would like to make it special."

"Yes, sir."

"I want everything to go off nice and sweet. Make sure the only people on the plane are our people, no non-company people. She must not know we are going to Paris, France until we walk out of that plane at Aéroport de Paris."

"Oh yes, sir," she said, with a smile. "I'll see that secrecy is maintained throughout."

"I'm going to give that girl the best three weeks of her little life. Make sure she has a credit card that's good in all the best stores, in Paris."

"I will, sir."

"And I want you to take care of that Granger boy. His parents were ambushed and killed by terrorists on the East Coast

Road. When he arrives, see to it that he gets everything he wants."

"Yes, sir."

The phone rang. "Enright."

The voice on the phone said, "Sorry, sir. This is Dixon at Changi."

"Well?"

"We may have a situation on our hands, sir."

"What do you mean, a situation?"

"Well, the isotopic transducer shows that ..." He stopped abruptly, and then continued. "Well quite a situation, sir. You should be here."

Mr. Enright put the phone down silently. "See to it that the car is out front in five minutes, Miss Yan."

"Yes, sir."

The term 'situation' is a code for something serious, anything serious. They had suffered terrorist attacks and sabotage before. He thought that's what it may be this time. He sat back in his chair and stroked his forehead again, then leaned forward and pressed the intercom button.

"How long would it take to get my helicopter here, Miss Yan?"

"I'll check, sir."

He let go the button and sat back. The last thing he needed was a situation when his daughter was coming for her surprise holiday. He sat staring into nowhere, thinking.

"Your helicopter is being serviced at Paya Lebar Airport, sir, and won't be ready for at least two hours. However, the Westland is already airborne and doing film work at Blackamatie," the girl's voice said on the intercom.

"How long would it take to get the Westland here?"

"About ten minutes, sir."

"See to it."

"Yes sir."

"Oh and cancel the car."

"Yes, sir."

He felt better now that the 'situation' was being attended to. He collected a couple of things and left the office "Miss Yan," he said on passing.

"Yes, sir?"

"See to it that my helicopter is ready as soon as possible and call Major Reeves. Tell him to stand by, we may need military assistance." He left for the helipad in the back parking lot. As he reached the area, the sound of the machine echoed in the distance. The aircraft arrived, touched down gently and the door opened. Enright walked at a crouch and climbed in.

"Sorry to call you off a job," Enright shouted. "Get me to the Changi plant and fast."

The helicopter lifted off and sped to Changi. In about ten minutes, he entered the factory from the roof-landing pad. Dixon stood waiting for him.

"Well?" Enright said as they entered the security of the building.

"I don't know what to make of it, sir, but the scanner is showing that the new man, Mr. Chan, and Sammy Sahananden are at sea."

"At sea, what the hell are they doing at sea?"

"Yes, we don't know sir."

"At sea? So how is this a situation?"

"Well, now they are twenty or thirty miles out and heading directly away from Singapore."

"Oh God! You mean they've been abducted."

"It looks that way, sir."

"We should dispatch a helicopter with troops A.S.A.P."

"Sorry, sir, it's impractical. They'll be out of scanner range anytime now."

"Get the big scanner online immediately."

"It already is sir." They reached the scanner room. "What's the exact position?" Dixon snapped to the operator.

"They've passed out of range, Mr. Dixon. Chan seems to still be aboard, but the other reflection has stopped," the operator said.

"They've cast him adrift. They only want Chan," Enright moaned. "Damn, I suppose we'll be getting some sort of ransom note soon. Get that helicopter off the roof and on its way to Sammy. I hope to God, they haven't harmed him."

The Westland rushed in the direction indicated by Dixon's men. While the helicopter made its way to investigate what had happened in the water almost fifty miles off the Changi shoreline, Mr. Enright demanded that secure communications be set up throughout his empire. Enright made himself at home and took charge of operations from what would have been Peter's office.

In only thirty minutes, the helicopter returned to the roof of the Changi plant. Mr. Enright waited patiently in his new office. A knock came to his door. "Come in."

Sammy walked in. He looked somewhat the worse for wear, his turban dishevelled and his clothes still wet. "I came to you first, sir. There are things that must be done."

"Glad to see you, Sammy," the boss-man said jumping to his feet to greet his employee.

"We were abducted, sir. They still have Dr. Chan. I do not know what they want with him. The boat we were on is the *Miasaki II*. I do not know who owns it, or where she is registered. I think it is a good thing to find all this out, sir. They looked like Koreans, many guns."

"You're a good man, Sammy. We'll get the buggers you can mark my words. Get yourself cleaned up, have a rest, but keep in touch. I'll get the ball rolling straight-away we must find that ship."

"Yes, sir."

Even before Sammy left the room, Enright was on the phone. "I want Major Reeves here A.S.A.P. with twenty hand-picked men for an airborne assault on a ship. Put the word out we are looking for the *Miasaki II*. Whatever port it stops in, I want to know. It's important you check the registry as well. I would like to know who owns that boat and her home port."

"Yes, sir, right away."

As he put the phone down, someone knocked on the door. "Come in."

"Do we have a stratagem to get Chan back, sir?" Mr. Dixon said entering the room.

"Yes, we do. We've got troops coming. I want the fastest ship in our fleet. What is it? Where is it? And how quick can you get it here?"

The SS Elizabeth is the fastest ship in the Enright fleet – a two-hundred-and-fifty-foot hydrofoil, capable of 55 knots. At the time needed, the vessel was in Pontianak in Borneo. Orders were given for her to sail immediately and with luck would reach Singapore by morning. Mr. Enright enjoyed the new challenge, something exciting he could get his teeth into. This time he intended to find and rout the enemy mercilessly.

The following day, Mr. Enright had returned to his own office in the headquarters building at Alexandra. A complete campaign was being planned to meet any eventuality. The newest toy, the Madecca satellite had been placed on standby. Its geo-stationary orbit directly above Singapore would permit secure communications on land and at sea. The S.S. Elizabeth arrived and after refuelling, awaited sailing orders.

Already they had found that the boat in question was registered in Libya, and belonged to an international playboy, Chow Peng. It was well known that Mr. Peng had liaisons with terrorist groups in Iran and the Middle East. The suspect was also well known to international authorities for smuggling, gunrunning, and a list of other crimes, though none had ever been proven.

Fifty mercenary troops were on their way down from Butterworth. Major Reeves and twenty crack troops standing by. The New Zealand Air Force arranged to send a Martin P6M-2 SeaMaster flying boat to be used for anything Enright wished. The whole operation waited and hinged on the sighting of the *Miasaki II*. Which occurred the evening of the third day, then things began to happen.

A report came in that the *Miasaki II* had been spotted

in Manila. The long-range scanner had been installed in the Elizabeth. Enright gave the order that no matter what, the *Miasaki II* must be followed until a boarding party could reach the ship. The Elizabeth departed with fifty assault troops. It would take almost twenty-four hours for her to reach Manila. No one in the Philippines had a scanner capable of checking to see if Peter was aboard the enemy boat.

In only four hours an agent with a small scanner arrived in the Philippine Islands. Already things were going wrong. They were unable to detect any reflectors aboard the *Miasaki II*. The agent reported the bad news to Singapore; they had already lost Peter Chan. In case the *Miasaki II* sailed unexpectedly, the Enright spy placed his own bracelet aboard. The Elizabeth would be able to track it from a range of forty to forty-five miles.

The *Miasaki II* left port only an hour after she had been marked by the Enright spy. Her direction was reported to the Elizabeth and a day and, a half later, sighted. The quarry made a heading south toward the Banda Sea. Tracking the vessel presented no problem as troops were standing by. About two days later, she stopped and dropped anchor near a small island on the outer fringe of the Banda Sea.

The report came into Singapore that Peter Chan's reflection had been detected on the island known as Dragon's Nest. The invasion force on the Elizabeth held back awaiting Mr. Enright to arrive on the scene. There seemed to be no hurry. The *Miasaki II* had been found, Peter had been found and the island hideaway identified. Mr. Enright decided to wait until he received word that his daughter had landed safely in Singapore before ordering the invasion.

The following day, the powerful scanner detected Endora's reflection at low altitude approaching Dragon's Nest Island. Unexpectedly the plane dived and crashed into the island. The scanner operator quickly established that Endora had survived the crash as her reflection moved about the crash site. Mr. Enright still in Singapore, had to be told the bad news and that there were also at least a couple of hundred enemy troops guarding the island.

"We must attack the place and rescue my daughter," bellowed Enright angrily.

"No," Major Reeves said. "We will have to use stealth and strategy. If we blunder onto that atoll, we'll probably get everybody killed including your daughter. We'll achieve nothing that way. Stealth and patience."

"Then what do you suggest, we just sit here and wait?"

Reeves stroked his moustache and stared blankly at the floor. "A commando raid. If we can get on the island without being noticed, a small force would do better than a large one. Once we've achieved our objective, then invade and eliminate the devils, once and for all."

"I like your thinking," Mr. Enright said. "The Kiwi plane will be here tomorrow. It is capable of landing on the water. This will be perfect. Major Reeves, hatch your plans. We are in your hands."

The following day, the Martin P6M-2 SeaMaster took to the sky with twenty combat troops, Major Reeves, Mr. Enright, Sammy, and a crew of four New Zealand airmen. Carefully directed by the Elizabeth through the Madecca satellite the plane manoeuvred at low altitude. It landed in the water on the far side of an adjacent island to the north of the Dragon's Nest Island. Two rubber Avon powerboats were inflated and cast into the water.

Three soldiers were left to guard the aircraft which remained silent and at anchor five hundred yards off the coast. Mr. Enright, Sammy, Major Reeves, and seventeen soldiers landed without opposition on the northern tip of Dragon's Nest Island. Quickly they set up camp and a scanner to search for his daughter and Peter. Endora Elizabeth was a mile and a half to the south and, like Peter, the signal varied in strength, indicating they had entered buildings or structures that impeded radio waves.

A scout party quickly began a search for the girl who appeared to be out in the open more than Peter, though even after two days they were unable to locate the exact position. The scout party returned to camp and the leader reported directly to Enright and Reeves in the tent. "I'm sorry, sir," he said. "But she seems to be inside the mountain. Whenever we approach the reflector enters the mountain, and we can't track her there."

"In the mountain?" Enright echoed.

"Yes, sir. The reflection came from solid rock. We could not find any entrance. Then as she penetrates deeper the signal vanishes. She must have climbed into some hidden cave, probably for refuge."

Suddenly, a man came running into the tent. "Sir, sir!"

"Yes?" Reeves said.

"We've spotted a flare, it's about a mile and a half to the south-west. Could have been on the beach."

"Was my daughter's reflector picked up?" Asked Enright.

"No sir. Whoever's on the beach, it's not your daughter."

"Send a party out there at once," Enright ordered, "whoever they are bring them in."

"Sir."

A small party of five men was immediately sent to investigate the flare sighting. It took them almost two hours to reach the reported area. On the way, they heard gunfire. Again no one was spotted and the scanner picking up a reading that led them to a solid cliff.

Mr. Enright became infuriated by their lack of success, the most advanced technology in the world, and they couldn't find a girl on a small tropical island. "Tomorrow, we'll move the whole party up the coast, and we'll search for this mysterious cave. By hook or crook we'll find a way in there."

By the next day, preparations were complete to begin the exploration of the island. "Don't you think it's rather funny?" Mr. Enright said. "We've never run across any enemy patrols, and there's supposed to be hundreds here, somewhere."

"Yes," Reeves said. "I'm beginning to think that the mountain is hollow. They must all be in there and believe they are undetectable and invulnerable."

"You're devious, Reeves," Enright said. "That's why I like you. If we can find the way in, will we have the advantage?"

"We sure will. With our firepower, we'll have them on the run."

"Good, I'm getting tired of being on the losing side. So far, they have had it all their own way."

"Not to worry sir. We'll overcome them soon."

Gunfire broke out up the eastern coast. Shortly after, heavy artillery fire began exploding midway up the island. The explosions could be seen from the camp and the artillery piece seemed to be out at sea and not visible from the land. Everyone was shocked; their mouths fell open in surprise as the giant laser fired from the top of the mountain. The artillery became silent, though the sound of small arms came closer and closer.

Unexpectedly, the Enright camp came under rifle fire. Reeves's men replied. One of the Avons got hit by machine-gun fire, the operator wounded and the boat deflated. The battle raged for some fifteen minutes and then the most unusual and amazing thing happened. A fifteen-foot golden robot appeared. It walked, knocking down small palm trees with its hands and stopped only two hundred feet from the camp perimeter.

"Hold your fire," Enright shouted. "Don't shoot."

THE DEATH SENTENCE

Chapter 17

As the portal closed, Peter found that he, Arjit and Horace were in a new corridor with steps leading down. The sound of terror and death permeated the air from behind the closed door.

"Are you going to cut me loose?" Friz said angrily.

Arjit raised his right leg and pulled a small knife from his sock. He sliced the rope holding Horace to Peter and the one rope between the lad's hands.

"Have you had that knife all along?" Peter asked.

"Indeed, my friend."

"You've had a weapon all this time?"

"Yes, would you have me use it and get us both killed?"

"I guess not."

With the ends of the rope still round each wrist, Horace ran down the long staircase. The door opened at the bottom and Friz stood in the doorway. "Come on," he yelled. "Don't stand around."

Peter and Arjit followed, down the steps and through the door. The portal closed. Quickly, Horace dashed to the door leading to the geothermal halls. The next door opened. As the two men approached the lad dashed down the spiral staircase. The two men blindly followed the boy down the stairs and into the long room, where clear water welled up into the stream. Horace ran the length of the very long room and at the end he pressed the luminous panel and opened the door to the next chamber.

The lad stood in the doorway facing the approaching men. Suddenly, he backed through the doorway, allowing the door to close. "Yes," he shouted excitedly. "Andrilla, do your thing. Kill the infestation."

The door opened and Arjit and Peter walked through. Horace glared at them, puzzled that they were alive. "You look surprised," Peter said.

"How did you open the door?"

"Pressed the luminescent plate, sure."

"You should be dead," Horace shouted. "You should be dead."

"No," Peter said. "I can open any door with a plate. Did you really think you could get rid of us that easily?"

"Andrilla should have killed you. You're the infestation."

"No, son, you've got it wrong. We're just prisoners. You tricked us all. You knew that those monsters would start, didn't you?"

"Yes. They'll kill all the infestation. They'll slaughter all the rotten dingoes that are a danger to the Andrilla."

"Quite a friendly kid," Peter said sarcastically. "Again, you're wrong son. Those troops have weapons. They'll soon destroy your robot friends. They've got rockets, armour piercers, the lot. Your friends will soon be laying in the dust, and then they'll come looking for us."

"The Terror bots can't be killed," Horace said his eyes filled with fire.

"Well, son," Peter said. "We must be friends, you and me. Somehow, we've got to survive. When they've destroyed those robot things, they'll cut through that door. When they get us, we'll be as dead as everything else on this island."

"Andrilla will kill them all, you'll see," Horace said. "The infestation will never get in here. Andrilla promised it would be the end if I started the Terror bots and I did."

"I hope you're right, kid. Can I speak with this Andrilla of yours?"

"Okay," Horace said. "I'll take you there."

Friz opened the door and they walked back to the half-round staircase. "What happened here?" Peter said looking at the bloodstains.

"It was my friend. The infestation caught her, but I saved her."

"Looks like a slaughterhouse, I don't think I've ever seen so much blood, what happened to this friend?"

"I told you the infestation caught us they tried to kill Lizzie."

Peter stroked his chin thoughtfully, still the rumbling of hostility echoed through the complex. "How long can we live in this place?"

"Not long," Horace said. "There are no toilets, no food, and only that water to drink." He walked up the stairs and into the corridor. Arjit and Peter followed the boy to the control room. "Sit there," he said, pointing.

Peter sat. Both he and Arjit were amazed at the similarity to the other control room they worked in. "Welcome, Dr. Chan," the Andrilla said.

"Hi," he replied weakly. "How did you know my name?"

Horace laughed as the Andrilla answered. "I am the Andrilla of this station. I monitor every room; I hear everything said in all languages."

"I see," Peter said, amused and surprised. "So you are the one that decides who can and cannot open doors."

"Yes. Non-reflectors are not permitted to open doors."

"Non-reflectors?"

"Your reflector is not working well, just as the girl and Arjit Singh's are not. I cannot identify you at a distance. You must be repaired."

"What exactly do you mean?"

"I know what he means," Horace said. "You'll have to go to the talon and have your reflector repaired. I did."

"Yes," the Andrilla said. "Both of you must report to the Talon. It will repair your reflector, then we shall talk again."

"I'll take you," Horace said jumping up excitedly.

"You're not going to try to get us killed again, are you?"

"No. If Andrilla trusts you, so do I." Horace led the way down the blood-soaked corridor to the medical room.

As they reached the door it opened and the sound of explosions echoed through the walls from a distance. The shockwave travelled through the rock and rattled things in the complex. There was not a trace of blood in the medical room, it looked as clean and sterile as the first time.

Peter stood awed by the medical room and its talon. The thunderous banging continued outside somewhere above them. "That's the girl you rescued?" He said walking over to her.

"Yes. Now stand in the circle. The talon will take care of you." Horace snapped.

Peter stood in the circle and the Talon came from its hiding place. As it hurried across the ceiling toward Peter, he took fright and retreated to the doorway.

"Chicken," Horace said. "It won't hurt you."

"Sorry, but I don't trust you kid."

"Andrilla told you to do it, not me."

Peter slowly advanced until he was in the circle. The Talon gently picked him up and carried him to the table next to Lizzie. The operation took only seconds. There was a dip in the lights and the terrible sound of the giant laser. The dragon began its breathing and wheezing quite audibly. Peter looked startled and pale as the machine released him.

Arjit took his place in the circle and received the same treatment. Both men had an instinctive fear of the mechanical device. Horace enjoyed the proceedings and eagerly bounced up and down with the excitement. While the device looked at Arjit, Peter walked to the girl. She tilted her head sideways and looked at him dreamily and then she smiled. "Hi."

"Hello sweetheart," he said softly. "How are you?"

She closed her eyes and returned to a sleep-like state.

Arjit's examined the spot on his arm where the Talon operated. "What happened to her?" he asked as they left the room.

"She was shot in the chest by the infestation."

"Why do you call them the infestation?" Peter inquired.

"Because they are. They shot Lizzie as we ran away from them."

"Poor little kid. And that machine performed surgery on her?"

"Yes."

Peter sat once again in the Andrilla chair. "Will that injured girl be okay?"

"Her wounds were not damaging to any vital organ; she lost a great quantity of blood. Yes, she will be alright."

"What were all those explosions we heard a little while ago?"

"A sea vehicle fired projectiles at a guardian."

"Then?"

"The laser was used to silence the sea vehicle."

"What happened to the guardians?"

"One is proceeding along the coast. It will destroy all the infestation and cleanse this island."

"This is totally unbelievable. Do you remember Corporal Miasaki?"

"Miasaki left here."

"Yes, he did. He didn't have a reflector; how come you didn't destroy him?"

"Miasaki's reflector was broken. He was one of the ancient ones from the sleep chamber."

Peter thought for a few seconds. "What about Arjit? He had no reflector?"

"He did when he entered with you."

"The necklace," Arjit said.

"Right, it's Enright's daughter." Peter smiled. "So we're all safe now, are we?"

"Safe? No, not safe. You must evacuate this station. Take the shuttle and fly to safety."

Peter looked at Arjit. "What shuttle?"

"You must use the shuttle and join the masters. You cannot stay," said the Andrilla.

"Cannot stay, why not?"

"Starting the guardians is the end. Their purpose is to defend while you escape."

"Then what?"

"Then they await the end."

Peter showed puzzlement on his face. "How long have you been here?"

"Five hundred forty-seven thousand, five hundred and nineteen days."

"Assuming 365 days to a year, how long's that approximately?"

"One thousand five hundred years."

"Holy mackerel," Peter said. "How long to the end?"

"Four hours and twenty minutes."

"Then what happens?"

"This island will be destroyed by a subterranean geological event that will annihilate everything above the water line and leave no trace."

"You must cancel that order. You've got to stop it," Peter said quite calmly.

"It is non-reversible. The process has been initiated. When the water reaches the magma dome, there will be an explosion that will lift this island a mile into the sky."

"Oh hell," Peter said, beginning to realize the trouble they were in. "Out of the frying pan, and into the magma dome."

"I think, my friend this is a problem beyond even your ingenuity," Arjit said.

"If we could get to the next island, would we stand a chance of survival?"

"No," the Andrilla said. "Every living thing within a hundred-mile radius will be destroyed. You must take the shuttle and the two masters that still sleep."

"There is no shuttle," Peter said. "You bloody fool machine, you've killed the lot of us."

"What of the others?" The Andrilla asked.

"Others, what others?"

"Those to the north," the machine replied.

Peter was confused, the Andrilla made little sense. "There are others to the north?"

"Yes."

"Are they good guys or bad guys?"

"They have clouded reflectors."

"Holy invasions!" Peter snapped. "We may yet have a chance."

"Why? What is it?" Arjit asked.

"I know what the machine is talking about. I know what a clouded reflector is. It explains everything. Have you got that necklace you took from the kid?"

"Yes," Arjit said, and pulled it from his pocket.

Peter laughed heartily. "Thank you, Mr. Enright," he shouted gleefully.

Horace snatched the necklace from Arjit. "That's Elizabeth's."

"Endora Elizabeth?" Peter asked.

"Yes."

"Arjit," Peter said excitedly. "You were right about God having a purpose for us all. The kid saved the girl, and she's saved us."

"I am filled with fear," Arjit said. "I feel that life is drawing to a close, yet you wish to cloud the air with mystery. Can we escape from here or not, and if so, why are we wasting time?"

"My friend, we can escape. Exactly how long have we got, Andrilla?" Peter said, already formulating a plan.

"Four hours and three minutes exactly."

Peter looked at his watch. "There's no time to waste. We'd

better get the hell out of here. If I'm right, we'll have no difficulty getting away from this place our salvation is at hand."

"What about the infestation?" Friz asked.

"The guardian will guide you to the north," the machine replied.

"Kid," Peter said. "Go get the girl. We've got to get out of here quickly. We've got to wake up the two in the sleep chamber and get them out of here too."

"No," the Andrilla said. "If there is no shuttle, they are to stay until the master returns. They are the old ones; it is their duty to remain."

"But they will die."

"Only in your eyes."

Horace ran to the medical room. "Lizzie," he yelled. "We've got to get out of here."

She lay quiet on the bench. The Talon had removed the feeding tube. She was still under the influence of a sedative. Dreamily, she rolled her head to see Horace. "Hi," she whispered.

"Come on, Lizzie. We got to get out of here. This place is going to blow up." He grabbed the new overalls from under the bench. "Come on, sit up, you've got to put this on." Trembling with anticipation, he gently helped her sit. The sheet fell off, exposing her completely naked body. For the first time, he could clearly see the terrible damage to her chest. The talon had neatly repaired the large, jagged hole, though it still looked terrible to Friz.

Struggling, he managed to get her legs into the overalls. "You'll have to stand," he said, trying to get her off the bench. With great difficulty, he managed to get the girl into the new clothes, she could not walk. He helped her back onto the bench.

"I'll get help," he said breathlessly. "Don't go away."

He rushed back to the control room. "You ready to go?" Peter asked.

"I can't move Lizzie. One of you will have to carry her."

DASH FOR FREEDOM

Chapter 18

Peter carried the girl piggyback style as they made their way to the chamber of the guardians. Andrilla opened the doors ahead of them. The guardian's chamber looked like a scene from hell. Exhausted, Peter put the girl down. Bodies and pieces of bodies lay all around mixed in with bent metal and rubble. One Guardian had remained and turned to face them, its forehead orifice glowing dangerously.

"That thing scares the hell out of me," Peter said breathlessly.

Taking the girl up again they walked to the already open elevator and when they entered, the Guardian followed. The door opened at the bottom, here the scene was little better. The wreckage of the little aircraft lay among the ruins and the dead soldiers. The outer door had been blasted open. Even outside, the view was no better. The camouflage had gone, the wooden jetty still burning; bodies littered the entire area.

The monster began walking north making way for the party to follow. Progress became slow and difficult, keeping up with the robot even harder. The group struggled against the difficult odds. Time was pressing and relentlessly running out.

"We must hurry," Peter said, straining under the extra weight of the limp girl.

With difficulty, Arjit took her from him. "Let me spell you a while, my friend."

Soon the bouncing and vibration lulled the girl into unconsciousness rendering her incapable of hanging on. Arjit had to adopt a different method of carrying her.

Checking his watch, Peter became agitated. Time was fleeting by and with it their chances of escape. At long last, and with less than three hours to go, they found the second Guardian and Major Reeves's camp. They were expected as Sammy had continuously monitored their progress on the scanner. When Peter and company arrived at the camp, both machines turned and walked back the way they come.

Arjit carried the unconscious girl over his shoulders, like a sack of potatoes. He went down to his knees as Peter and a nearby soldier helped lift the girl off. Enright emerged to greet the newcomers. "Welcome back," he said to Peter on approaching.

"Thank God it's you. We gambled it would be," Peter said.

"You've saved my daughter. How is she? What happened?" He leaned over the prostrate girl to get a better look.

"Yes, your daughter?" Peter said slowly. "She'll be okay. She was shot. We've got to get out of here. Now! I mean like, fast."

"Shot?" Enright said raising his voice in anger. "Shot by whom?"

"They're all dead and so will we be if we don't get the hell out of here and fast."

"We should get her to the plane," Enright said to Major Reeves. He turned to Peter. "So what's all this about? Is something chasing you? What about those machines, robots?"

"You're Lizzie's dad?" Horace said.

"Yes."

"So you're the one who caused all the trouble. You got us shot down by the drug lords," Horace said angrily.

"What are you burbling about, boy?"

"The box of heroin they loaded on the plane in Darwin. That's what they wanted. That's why they shot us down."

Enright smiled. "That was alumina. They make polishing paste to polish the glass in the lens factory with it. And who shot you down?"

"Well, you owe me a video game anyway," Horace said angrily.

"This entire island is about to become molten seismic dust," Peter said, interrupting. "We have to be better than a hundred miles from here in less than three hours. Now can we go? Like now?"

"Are you sure?"

"I have never been more certain of anything. I'll explain everything, but first let's get out of here. The Koreans are all dead, and this place is ready to blow, please let's make tracks."

Sammy walked forward. "Greetings, friend."

"Sammy!" Peter said in shock. "How did you get here? I thought you died in the sea."

Sammy laughed. "I am not that easy to kill. I thought that the *Miasaki II* would be doing better than a thousand feet a minute. In that case, I figured if I stayed under the water for half a minute, they would be too far away to hit me. I was right, and bullets do not travel well underwater. You see, here I am."

"How did you get out of the sea? You couldn't swim home from there."

"They were watching us on the scanner and came for us. But you had gone when they arrived."

"Well," Peter said. "I'm excited to see you, but if we don't get moving, there won't be any tomorrow."

"We've only got one boat, which means two trips to get to the plane," Mr. Enright said. "I'll tell the Elizabeth to make a run for it. She should be well clear of here at zero hour."

"We must all hurry," Peter snapped, "This entire island will blow up in two hours and forty-nine minutes. Where's the plane?"

"It's on the other side of that distant island, an hour's boat ride from here. But now we have only one Avon. The enemy destroyed the other one. Some of us will have to stay behind."

Peter looked shocked. "An hour there, an hour back, and an hour there again. There isn't time. Can't we shorten it somehow?"

"Maybe," Enright said thoughtfully. "Potentially. Take my daughter and as many men as possible. If you can't make it back in time, leave. Leave without us. Don't risk my daughter's life to save us."

"Then I'll stay," Peter said and began ushering others aboard the Avon.

Sammy went with Lizzie and Horace but Arjit refused to leave. Peter felt terrible. He sat on a fallen palm tree and watched as the Avon sped into the distance.

Mr. Enright sat beside him. "I could call the Elizabeth and have her diverted. She could be here in an hour."

"Wouldn't help," Peter said dolefully. "Not enough time for the getaway. Besides, I wouldn't want to be responsible for anyone else's death. Why didn't you go with Sammy? After all, you're the boss."

"Endora Elizabeth is my life. If I die here, it doesn't matter. But if I leave here others will die in my place. Endora would never forgive me. This way I'll be a hero, and she'll be the lord of the manor. Sammy will care for her for as long as he lives."

"Well," Peter said with a sigh, "I guess I'll be keeping you company."

"You're a good man, Peter. I wish I had longer to get to know you."

"I could give you a conducted tour of the Andrilla complex. Take us about an hour to get there."

"No, we'll remain here until the last, just in case they get better speed out of the Avon. It will be coming back empty. What's this Andrilla thing?"

Peter put his hand in his pocket and pulled out one of the magical cubes. "Now I know how it works. The whole thing has become academic. Would you believe it works on a principle very similar to your locating scanner?"

"If you say so. What is it?"

"That's how we survived. The Andrilla recognized the isotopic reflector as friendly. That's why the robot didn't destroy your party they thought you were of the ancient ones."

"I still don't know what an Andrilla is or what your talking about."

"Well, to be truthful, neither do I. For some reason, about one and a half millennia ago, some aliens built a receiving station. They used geothermal energy. This island was the perfect spot. I don't know what they were doing here, but some of them are still here and will die when the island blows. The rest of them were recalled and went back to wherever they came from. They obviously intended to return to this place. The Andrilla's capable of running everything unaided, so it was left on autopilot so to speak."

"But what's its purpose?"

"I asked the Andrilla that question."

"Explain."

Peter stroked his chin deep in thought. "The place is some form of advance outpost. It was built by aliens to keep on eye on their experiments here on earth. I guess maybe we are their experiments."

Enright smiled. "Aliens, eh?"

"Yeah. They identify their own people by a reflector inserted under the skin. The Andrilla's like a giant scanner and can detect and identify people at a great range."

"What, like our reflectors?"

"Exactly. It read my reflector and thought I was one of them. You wouldn't believe what happens to people who don't have a reflector. Those giant robots were started by a lad called Horace, the one who saved your daughter's life. They terminated the station, and anything that hasn't got a reflector. Now they are just waiting for the big bang."

"What is this big bang?"

"I don't fully understand it, but they originally diverted an underground river. There's a huge magma dome, that's what caused this island in the first place. Well, the diversion equipment has been destroyed, so when the water level reaches the right height, it will pour into the dome. The resulting explosion will lift this island almost into orbit. Tidal waves, shock waves, and tsunami. Devastation that's going to make Krakatoa look like a hiccup."

"Wow," Enright said, "and we're in the epicentre."

The Avon pulled up to the open back doors of the huge flying boat. The process of unloading and refuelling began. Sammy looked at his watch only one hour and thirty-three minutes left. There was little or no point returning for the others in the Avon. Struck with a sudden impulse he ran to the other end of the great open chamber and up the ladder onto the flight deck.

"Captain," Sammy said excitedly. "How long to start the engines?"

"It'll take about ten minutes to get the first one fired up, then the rest within five minutes. However, it'll take about fifteen minutes running to get full thrust and temperature."

Sammy was performing mental arithmetic. "How fast can this thing taxi in the water?"

"Up to takeoff speed."

"No, what I mean is, how fast can you safely taxi to any given position?"

"Oh, maybe fifty, sixty, knots."

As if a light had been turned on in Sammy's head, he jumped to attention. "Start those engines captain, now." He jumped on the ladder and slid to the bottom with a bang. He rushed to the loading dock. "Never mind the fuel, get everybody off that Avon and tie it up. We are going to use the plane." Quickly he rushed back to the flight deck. "Captain, let's go." He pointed to the chart. "I want you to get this plane to the north end of that island fast. Now. Lives depend on it."

With less than an hour left, Mr. Enright looked at Peter. "I don't think they'll come. There's no time left."

Peter looked at his watch. "We've still got fifty-seventy minutes. Look!" he exclaimed, jumping up.

Instantly a cheer went up from the soldiers and all present on the beach. The flying boat came into view heading in their direction. Arjit smiled a sardonic smile. "So," he said. "God shows his hand at last. We are saved my friend, we are saved."

The Avon quickly came ashore and collected the stragglers. On arrival back at the plane, the rubber boat was unloaded and cut adrift. The big door closed as the engines of the airplane began to scream. The machine started its takeoff directly away from the island, though time was swiftly running out.

Enright shouted orders to Sammy. "Get this aircraft out o' here. Don't bother with altitude, we need speed. Put the greatest distance between us and that island as fast as possible."

Sammy rushed and gave the orders to the pilot while Enright walked to an observation window. His heart pounded as he craned to see the island slowly disappear into the distance. The plane took to the air and began gaining speed. "It's going to be close," Enright said looking at his watch.

Peter joined him at the window. "Next on my list of priorities is to find Monique, my fiancée."

"Why, is she lost?"

"Chow Peng said he had her prisoner somewhere."

Mr. Enright laughed. "He lied. At this very minute, she is on her way out to Singapore. She thinks she's going to help look for you."

Peter smiled with relief. "I hope this plane can take the shock wave."

"Yes. Well, I guess we'll soon know."

Almost like a dream sequence Enright watched as the island exploded. A giant plume shot into the sky with an ever-growing mushroom cloud. The shock wave dashed across the water at the speed of sound like an expanding bubble. It flattened the water as it rushed toward the fleeing aircraft.

"Hang on everyone," shouted Mr. Enright.

The shock wave hit. It felt as though the plane had struck

solid ground. Then the machine fell several hundred feet as it dropped into the depression that followed the shock wave. It was all over, the plane survived with little damage. Enright felt exhausted as he looked at his men huddled around inside the bay. A warm feeling of relief flushed over him.

"Thank God, for that," he said to Peter.

Enright walked to his daughter who was lying on an upturned inflated dinghy. Kneeling, he said, "Hello, my darling. We'll get you home soon."

She opened her eyes. "Hi, daddy. You came for me; you came for me!"

"Yes, my love, I came for you."

Horace was sitting on the floor of the aircraft beside her and holding her hand. His face was flushed with excitement. "Wow," he said. "This is the most exciting holiday I've ever had."

VISIT MY WEBSITE AT

www.wentworth-m-johnson.com

ABOUT THE AUTHOR

Wentworth M Johnson

Wentworth M Johnson (born 1939) is a Canadian writer of many science fiction and mystery adventure novels. He was born in the town of March, Cambridgeshire, England. W.M. Johnson is the great grandson of William Edward Bourne 1851-1925 (Playwright, dramatist, and theatrical producer). Johnson has  published newspaper and magazine articles, as well as fiction and non-fiction books. In the RAF Wentworth M Johnson worked with the Gurkha regiment reclaiming Borneo after it had been invaded by Indonesia and later as navigator with 1125 Marine Craft unit, chasing pirates in the South China Sea. Spent two years in Nairobi on international communications and handed the small station over to the Kenyan Army. Leaving the Royal Air Force in 1967 Wentworth M Johnson immigrated to Canada and worked in a lumber factory for a short while. He then spent five years working in a munitions factory and laboratory. After a disagreement with the boss, he walked out and immediately got a job with a local television station and worked there for some twenty-eight years, until taking early retirement in the year 2000. Since his retirement Wentworth M Johnson has spent his time building flying scale model aircraft, playing the Bagpipes and several other woodwind instruments, collecting British postage stamps and of course he has continued to write. As an author Wentworth M Johnson's lifelong passions have been writing and English history from Roman times to the present.

BOOKS BY THIS AUTHOR

The Angel Of The Vail

Investigating the mystery of the sudden and unexplained appearance of three dead bodies on an English moor an intrepid explorer becomes embroiled in the strangest mystery of all times. Lurking in the Valley of the Vail is the deadly answer for all to find.

Without delay the Scot ran into the Vail. All was silent. The sound of clashing swords had gone. Not even a bird whistled. It was a damp and dismal day; fog rolled in over the rocks where the battle had been. There were no bodies, no sign of a fight at all ...

Sideways Time - How I Discovered The Universe

Beyond the limits of known space there lies an empire where the Septains rule. Ganga, a creature that looks despicable to humankind operates his little sub-empire on his own planet he calls Gangora. Ganga the Septain collects intellectual artifacts - a sort of interplanetary hobby. Supported by the mineral riches of his planet, he buys, steals, and cunningly inherits that which interests him most. Ganga ineffectively tries to steal the secret of temporal travel form a pair of foolish Fargasoids. Having failed he turns his attention to the perfect android. Without morals or even common decency, Ganga covets all he surveys until an Earthling known as Johnling Peterson visits him.

Happisburgh High-Jinks

John is a retired detective from Ontario Canada while Amy has the unusual abilities of a feline-whisperer - she can actually communicate with domestic cats at a primitive level. Paintings begin to go missing from a private art collection when Amy and John Cotton take an all expenses paid holiday in North Norfolk. Skulduggery and mischief are afoot as the Lord of the Manor tries to ensure his heritage. Suddenly a serving girl who is also an artist's model is murdered and Lord Wessley is framed. The murder throws the household into confusion and the Lord is arrested. The art theft appears to be an impossibility; thus the police are not convinced such an event ever took place. The murder on the other hand seems quite obvious.

The Curse Of Valdi

Matthew Adams is a Canadian and whilst suffering monetary difficulties he suddenly becomes the heir to what is known as the Edict. On offer is a huge and mysterious estate in the peaceful countryside of Norfolk England. Matthew's only daughter is troublesome and at that awkward age of being neither adult nor child. Moving into the huge empty house the girl begins to learn things that should only belong in the past. Colette sees the ghosts and accepts them as part of her extended family. Unable to see the ethereal residents for themselves both her mother and father become increasingly worried for the girl's sanity and safety. Matthew's only hope is to find the reason for the haunting and unravel the secrets of the white lady. The all-terrifying Shee devil must be faced and then banished from the estate.

The Beast Of St John's Cove

The legend says that St. Bedric slew the griffin and gave

prosperity to all the Christian people of the area. It is written that keeping the faith and remembering the griffin will maintain wealth and happiness for all. But does it? In truth the legend becomes the excuse for wholesale slaughter, degradation and enslavement. By pure chance one man, who should have died, finds himself the only survivor of an inhuman massacre. An all-consuming evil has engulfed St. John's Cove leaving only this one living human to solve the riddle.

Through The Apple Store

It seems that someone has murdered an actress. Who would believe the actual truth? Howard thinks a wandering Viking is the guilty party and Donavon Merryville gets the blame. In order to appease mad Albert and solve the murder, Donavon enters on a fantastic voyage through the centuries. He discovers and falls in love with Anneke, a siren from the 1800s. Forced by Albert, driven by love and inexorably channelled by time itself, Don blunders into the Viking wars of East Anglia and discovers a plot to assassinate Winston Churchill, the wartime English Prime Minister. Will he stop the cycle and who will get the blame for the murder of an actress.

Imps Of Willow Dell - Adventures In Time

Three people vanish without a trace in a sleepy little farm community; legend has it that they were taken by the Devil. A haunted hill, a deserted ruin and three children with vivid imaginations conspire to unravel the mystery ... yet something sinister is lurking in those parts. Alice, a retired schoolteacher, defends the children and her beliefs to the point of near ruination, though some say she is only shielding a murderer. A haunted hill, a deserted ruin, and three children with vivid imaginations connive to create a fun and a fear-filled adventure that no one will forget. The Devil snatches Sonyi and the boys move heaven and lots of earth to find her.

The Horror Of Craigai   Auk Authors

In olden times an alien craft crashed in the sea not far from Edinburgh. Its only surviving passenger burrowed into the ground and took up permanent residence. This deadly parasite from outer space controls all it surveys while the human population, its food, is unaware of the creature's existence. In modern times a small self-appointed team of ne'er-do-wells take on the impossible task of saving the world. Unknown to almost all of humanity this horror resides in subterranean darkness beneath a Scottish moor. Armed only with guts, wits and a peculiar device called the PXI the human heroes try to unravel a centuries old mystery. Is it possible for a mere human to penetrate the dark secrets of an alien being? Can man overcome the stupendous odds? Living on a diet of dissolved human flesh the alien creature blinds its victims to reality by using a mind-bending psycho-control. Inevitably there are people who are immune to the hypnotic influence of the alien—they have to be eliminated or at least neutralized.

THE ADVENTURES OF TWO SPECIAL ANIMALS

Trilogy: 1: A Dual Tale   2: The Secret of Castle Duncan   3: Trouble at Castle Duncan
Fun for the whole family from youngster to grandparents.

A Dual Tale

The Adventures of Two Special Animals book 1
The first in a series of three; it is new different, exciting and all about two very dissimilar but lovable animals. Dragons do not exist! Hmm, or do they? Everyone knows that cats cannot speak, or can they? An endearing story of two most unlikely creatures and an explanation as to how they came into existence. Hilatus flies the Spanish Main and attacks a gold carrier aiding the pirates in their nefarious work. Minette escapes her fate by sailing to the Americas only to be shipwrecked.

The Secret Of Castle Duncan

The Adventures of Two Special Animals book 2
What if you were to come face to face with a real live fire-breathing dragon? Ridiculous! Maybe and maybe not. Something fearful lives in the dungeons of the old castle, something so terrible as to scare mere humans near to death. Thirteen-year-old Jimmy not only knows what it is and where it is, he's the one responsible for it being there. Few people have actually seen it, and those who have, fear to mention it. 'The Secret of Castle Duncan,' is a romping adventure feasibly encountering the

infeasible and reasonably explaining the inexplicable. A young lad of thirteen years discovers the impossible, a living lesser green dragon.

Trouble At Castle Duncan

The Adventures of Two Special Animals book 3
Minette is kidnapped and held for ransom by Malcolm Macbeth. Jimmy confers with Jessica and decides to try duping the bad guy by substituting the diamonds. The criminal, not being stupid substitutes the cat. Jimmy is snatched from the beach in reprisal and a threatening call is made to the castle. The bad guys have no idea what they are up against. The Cummings family is no ordinary bunch of Americans. Malcolm Macbeth is trying to branch out on his own. He holds Jimmy and the cat in an old disused lighthouse north of the Isle of Skye. Jessica followed by Alistair and Valerie come to the rescue.

BILL REYNER MYSTERY ADVENTURES

Bill is the reluctant hero with the Midas touch. He is tall, powerfully built and quick to action. He is basically lazy and would prefer to stay at home, but Gran always manages to fire up his dynamo.

Before writing any Bill Reyner story I actually go there, the very places where the action takes place. Sometimes I change the names, as they say, 'to protect the innocent.'

There is nothing like the ambience of reality to encourage imaginary actions.

Fiend's Gold

A Bill Reyner Mystery Adventure Book 1

A couple of hundred years ago, a wild and unruly family fell upon a floundering ship filled with gold. Gold fever and bandits destroyed the Fiend family, but through their cunning the treasure was hidden and remained that way for almost 200 years. Edgar Reyner, a multi-millionaire, bought the island reputed to be the hiding place of Fiend's gold. He, too, became a victim of gold fever and was killed for his efforts. Edgar left the bulk of his estate to his unruly and lazy nephew William Reyner (Bill). William Reyner and his grandmother visit a lawyer in a Northern Ontario town, where they become the heirs to the Reyner fortune. Bill visits his new island and learns of the mysteries and ghosts that inhabit the lonely outpost. Overcome by the island's tranquility and beauty, he makes the fatal decision to hunt for the long-lost treasure.

Mania

A Bill Reyner Mystery Adventure Book 2
Prompted by the unearthing of a human skull in the woods near his house, Bill Reyner begins an investigation into a 20-year-old unsolved murder. Unlike the police, he becomes involved with the characters associated with the deed. His entanglement deepens, as does his knowledge of the case. Joining the deadly and insane cult, he intends to trap them, only to find the tables are turned and he becomes the quarry. At every turn, the Mania is ahead of him. With full knowledge of their actions but no physical evidence, he has nowhere to hide and no one to call for help.
Bill's only option is to fight them on their own terms.

Edinburgh Cuckoos

A Bill Reyner Mystery Adventure Book 3
Summoned to England by his ex-girlfriend, Bill Reyner and his associate North try to kill two birds with one stone – a short holiday and very quick investigation. A simple missing person case couldn't possibly turn out nasty – or could it? Whilst retracing the steps of a missing woman, Bill accidentally uncovers an incredibly diabolical organization that has existed for years. It soon becomes evident that while he is searching for the long dead and dear departed; someone behind the scene is manipulating his every move. What could wax figures, picturesque castles and alluring Scottish damsels possibly have to do with missing people?

Damp Graves

A Bill Reyner Mystery Adventure Book 4
Lost in the bowels of the earth, Bill and Newf find the unimaginable controlled by the unassailable – and hidden well

enough to be almost undiscoverable. How could a house, a graveyard, a cave and a hospital all be so closely related? To save lives the puzzle has to be unravelled, and quickly. A fair maiden is being held firmly in the jaws of hell and Bill's task is to rescue her, but he is outsmarted at every turn. He tries to match wits with an evil genius, only to discover he is playing right into the monster's hands.

Lions And Christians

A Bill Reyner Mystery Adventure Book 5
Bill takes a paid holiday at a hunting lodge in northern Ontario. Is it a paradise with everything a rich man could ever dream of? Behind the pleasure stirs the hand of the very devil himself, offering only misery and murder. Inexorably drawn into a bizarre trap, Bill starts a revolution in an attempt to avoid death and disaster and in so doing finds yet another hidden treasure.

www.ingramcontent.com/pod-product-compliance
Lightning Source LLC
Chambersburg PA
CBHW060225180626
46813CB00007B/2964